I0666525

No Place To Go

JOHN H. SIME

Lovstad Publishing
www.Lovstadpublishing.com

Copyright © 2015 John H. Sime
All rights reserved. No part of this book
may be reproduced or transmitted
by any means without written
permission from the author.

NO PLACE TO GO
First Edition

ISBN: 0692478388
ISBN-13: 978-0692478387

Printed in the United States of America

Cover design by Lovstad Publishing

For my wife, Jan

NO PLACE TO GO

Prologue:
Saturday, Oct. 24, 1953
6:58 P.M.

...Beyond a ridgeline, which overlooked the City of La Crosse, Wisconsin, a silver-colored, crescent shaped craft hovered below treetop level. It was a few feet above an enormous, recently-harvested hayfield surrounded on all sides by tall trees. Inside the craft, a very tall, green-skinned, Reptilian figure stood in a circular chamber and faced control panels. The Reptile on two legs was surrounded by smaller, large headed, gray skinned, semi-humanoid creatures. They all watched images which were projected onto thin air, as if in a hologram ...images of certain human beings now in the city below: Cy Butt, the Master, Bernard, Ned Lein, and Madeline Marley...

Chapter 1
Thursday, October 29, 1953
La Crosse, Wis.

"It's not true that we have no place to go." said La Crosse, Wisconsin police chief, George Lewis (forefinger nervously wrestling collar, noted Philio).

Philio DeGarmo, tall, gawky, crew-cut, fresh out of law school, heard these words. He watched as like fresh-picked fruit, they went into the grubby, hip-pocket notebook owned by Nels Nelson--the still young, but balding reporter of the *La Crosse Tribune*. Philio, upon the orders of his boss, Wisconsin Attorney General Grover W. Townsend, was there to study the event and keep an eye on one of their contacts in La Crosse.

Jammed together in the dingy, drafty press room, deep beneath the dome of the fortress- like courthouse of the County of La Crosse, Wisconsin was Nelson, and a mob of other reporters from throughout the Midwest and the nation as a whole The soot blackened dome would be torn down in 1965 and replaced by a

Stalinesque hall of bureaucracy. In 1953, it was still 19th century, classically ornamented, Midwestern railroad town rococo stone work that the seekers of law and order had to deal with in City of La Crosse.

The overcast sunlight (gray as a dead man's eyes) filtered through the huge, double hung windows. It barely reflected the ash-strewn and tobacco-spat stone tile floor.

This was a cold and windy Thursday afternoon. It was now five days since the ghastly, mysterious disappearance of fifteen-year-old baby sitter Madeline Marley.

She had been taken from a ranch style home in La Crosse's newly-developed eastern addition, at the base of the towering landmark, Grand Dad's Bluff, which itself was almost iconic of the city. Beneath this commanding bluff, the City of La Crosse half-moons outward from the eastern bank of the Mississippi River. About 50,000 people live on the alluvial plain between the huge river and the rock escarpment-topped bluffs.

The night in question had been Saturday, Oct. 24, 1953. It was Homecoming night at La Crosse State University and night of a big game. Professor and Mrs. Arvid Magnussen decided to attend the game with their good friends and his English Department colleague, Professor and Mrs. Norman Marley. The Magnussens hired the daughter of the Marleys, the young Madeline, to baby-sit 20 month old Theresa. When they returned from the game to retrieve their daughter at the Marley home, they found their baby unharmed, but they also found Madeline missing. Everyone tried to untangle the unravel-able mystery (which, eventually did happen, although the results were classified.)

Philio watched Nels scribble a few lines into his notebook as Chief Lewis delivered his statements and answered questions from the reporters. But these were almost always the same lines he had scribbled day after day for nearly a week--no progress, no news. After the press conference, Nels headed over to one of his favorite watering holes--The Coo-Coo Club on Jay Street. Philio naturally followed him, but at some distance. This was a small establishment run by a husband and wife, named Sterling, with a rare sense of humor. A siren device and bells went off as patrons entered the door. A heating grate in the floor concealed an air blower, which could be set off by the bartender whenever women in skirts stood over it. The walls were solidly covered with cartoons, paintings of dogs playing cards, raucous jokes. An Egyptian mummy case stood in an alcove. The door to this case could be opened by a button behind the bar, revealing a mummy in bandages and top hat.

When Philio entered the establishment, he noticed that Nels Nelson was already huddled with Cy Butt, the very man DeGarmo had come to town to keep an eye on, and so, he slipped in quietly and sat back against the wall, watching his two targets.

The first person Nels noticed as soon as he entered the Coo-Coo Club was certainly Cy Butt. Now, sometimes, Nels might have just turned around and headed back outside in order to avoid being in the same bar with this decadent scion of a Viroqua, Wis. pioneer family. But, sometimes Nels sought the *bon vivant* out. And this was one of those times. Cy Butt was well known in every bar within a hundred miles of Viroqua. He was a professional student at the University of

Wisconsin in Madison, which he had attended on a family inheritance for decades. Somewhere along the line he actually became a lawyer, and for a while in the 1950s he worked part-time in the office of the State Attorney General. In the years after his death in 1968, he would be written up in more than one history of the University and remembered as a sort of quaint joke, a memorable symbol of the wild life of Madison. Nels, however, himself a native of Viroqua, knew that there was a more tragic side to Cy Butt. Butt was described by bartenders as "a bottle a day man". While he was never violent under the influence of alcohol, Cy was well known to concoct elaborate jokes, stunts, and to compose sharp tongued letters to the editor.

But, now, Cy was probably just what Nels needed after a week of depressing news about the disappearance of Madeline Marley. All of La Crosse was walking about in a numb stupor. How could such a thing happen in this placid city next to the Mississippi? Chicago, yes, Madison, maybe, but La Crosse-- impossible. And Nels could now detect the growing signs of hysteria. A crackdown seemed to be yearned for. Cy had talked about how the mentality of Sen. Joe McCarthy seemed to be lurking about the streets. Nels found that kind of talk risky. Nevertheless, cars were being searched by gas station attendants and plastered with "I'm O.K." stickers. Those who refused were turned over to the police.

So, when Nels saw Cy But on one of the stools of the Coo Coo Club-- lounging-- (despite the danger) he headed right for him. As was his custom in all bars, Cy Butt was seated near the bathroom. He did this because after decades of dedicated drinking his kidneys

4

were beginning to give out on him. He also did it because the bathroom served as a good location for him to prepare his sometimes-disgusting practical jokes. These included jokes such as his legendary smearing of peanut butter on a toilet seat in order to pass it off to an unwitting bartender as some loathsome toilet accident. Then in mock outrage Cy demands that it be cleaned up, while reaching down with his bony index finger to scoop up some of the offal and wag it under the nose of the bartender. Then Cy would conclude the performance by sticking the brown glob in his mouth. Bartenders more than once vomited on the spot, making Cy's triumph all the more complete, as he struts out of the toilet cackling like a rooster. Only his generous cash tips to the bartenders enabled Cy to get back into some bars after such stunts. And the painful thought of some of those jokes was in the mind of Nels as he approached the skinny, hunched-over, slightly built figure crouching like an alley cat, eyes 3/4 shut, but still watching, also like a cat.

"Well howdy doody there Nels, old boy, pull up a bar stool and have one on me." Cy motioned the bartender: "Barkeep, get me another glass of I.W. Harper, with water, no ice, and get Mr. Nelson a wee dram as well."

"Gimme a Peerless beer, John." said Nels to Mr. Sterling, the owner of the club. "Thank you Cy. Don't mind if I do. It's been a hell of a rough day."

"Been over at Lewis's press conference I presume?" said Cy.

"That's right. This time no news is bad news." responded Nels.

"They won't ever find her." said Cy.

"What makes you say that? She's probably walking

5

the streets of Tijuana right now with some Army deserter boyfriend." replied Nels with a firm nod.

"I don't think she is. I think where she is she'll never come back from." grinned Cy.

"Well, they'll probably find her body. They need to start dragging the river." said Nels, smiling with a touch of condescension.

"That won't do a bit of good. She is not to be found." grinned Cy.

Nels let that remark fall into silence as the bartender brought Cy's whiskey and Nels' beer. The way the old drunk said those words with such certainty generated a measure of concern--was he somehow involved? So, finally, Nels could resist no longer and asked:

"Cy, do you know something about the case?"

"Only that she was kidnapped by a gangster named Bernard."

"What?"

"He went over there with a weird old farmer named Ned Lein to kidnap her. Dragged her out of the house. Took her away in a car parked up the street a ways. Drove her out of town, then a flying saucer came down and took her away, and one of the aliens shot a paralyzing ray..." Cy paused, as if reflecting upon something painful.

It took a few seconds for the full measure of this performance to sink into Nels. But he soon was laughing uproariously.

"By God, Cy. You really had me going there. I was almost believing that stuff there for a while. You oughta be careful here in this town talking like that now. Some people in La Crosse don't think that type of joke is real funny right now."

Cy replied: "The trouble is kid--it ain't no joke."

It was when Philio heard this remark that he rose and walked across the bar room to intercept Cy before he began to babble drunkenly about aliens, and flying saucers, and a whole host of other things that F.B.I. agents had sternly cautioned them to say nothing about. Plus, he was not altogether sure about Nels Nelson. Philio had learned that Nels was a member of the old Wisconsin Progressive Party. It was Philio's job to know this type of thing about the people who hung around Cy Butt. Cy of course, knew Philio was coming without even turning his skinny, hunched figure around and looking:

"Howdy doody there Philio, why'nt ya start being sociable and come sit with us instead of being such a wall flower?..." said Cy, turning around and giving Philio a broad wink.

Chapter 2
Monday, October 5, 1953
La Crosse, Wis.

Madeline Marley had dreamed again last night of becoming a nun. But she didn't think she really wanted to be one--particularly because she was a Methodist.

She had known Catholic girls here in La Crosse who had become nuns. Or at least she had seen them in the hallways at Central High School, and heard the other kids talk about them. What she most envied these girls was the sense that: "The running is over." That phrase ran through her fifteen-year-old mind often. That was what she wanted--the running to be over. To be in the place she needed to be.

Madeline crossed Losey Boulevard on the far east edge of La Crosse. She headed west toward Central High School. She crossed the street near the vacant field, which would within fifteen years see the construction of the a new Central High School. But now, in Fall, 1953, this neighborhood where Madeline

Marley lived was on the edge of a frontier--the frontier of the post war 50s of ranch style houses, subdivisions with winding streets, tiny saplings looking forward to a future as spreading shade trees adorning the retirement years of the young parents who made this new territory their own. Madeline crossed Losey Boulevard and headed into the past of La Crosse. She passed the houses and businesses built in the early 20th century and 19th century. She headed to the stately brick edifice of the then Central High School, built in 1907. Sometimes Madeline regretted her parents' choice to build in a new subdivision, beyond the cozy, tree-lined, neighborhoods of central La Crosse. She sometimes felt too exposed, like a delicate flower on a stark plain, not quite rooted in her era. She loved the oldness of the brick mansions, stone churches, ornate Victorian porches which she passed as she walked to school. She loved that safety of a known goodness. She sometimes feared the unknown newness of subdivisions such as her own. The limestone bluffs and the pine shrouded woods at the top of the bluffs almost seemed to be too close for comfort. She felt safer as she got closer to the old downtown and the Mississippi River.

Block after block, Madeline walked west towards her high school, and so intent she was upon her destination that she did not notice at all the battered, black 1938 model Ford farm truck, with an unpainted wooden box. A thoroughly nondescript vehicle, driven by an unimpressive, unshaven man wearing a grimy baseball cap--the truck passed by Madeline more than once, approaching her from different angles, once slowing almost to a dead stop as if the driver were consulting a map. Farm trucks of this sort were boringly frequent in market town La Crosse, meriting scarcely a side-glance, even by the local police--who sought sportier game in the form of speeding Buicks and Cadillacs.

And as the trees Madeline passed turned into the tall, stately, old-rooted veterans planted at the turn of the century and the younger, middle-aged trees planted in the Roaring Twenties, she began to think about Paris, and hum her favorite song about Paris: "The last time I saw Paris," Madeline had never seen Paris, but she so yearned to go there, and go to so many other places far off. Places far off from La Crosse, and her new subdivision on the new side of Losey Boulevard, where none of the trees were more than 3 feet tall, and all of the houses were one story, low to the ground. No towers, no crenulations, no soul.

Even though the subdivision was a very new thing on the American scene, fifteen-year-old Madeline Marley was already an acute observer and critic of the phenomenon, and she had found it soul killing and lacking. It would still be almost five years before popular authors such as Norman Mailer and Vance Packard would zero in on the subdivision as a setting for a new archetypal American tragedy. But Madeline Marley could have told them all that very same stuff in 1953, if anybody had bothered to ask her. Which mostly people didn't. Nobody doubted that Madeline had the answers. A lot of people just didn't want to ask the questions--like boys and some teachers.

The battered Ford truck continued to stalk Madeline as she approached Central High School. The driver was a fiftyish, largely toothless man, who looked from a distance like a farmer, but who upon closer approach exuded not the wholesome aroma of the cow barn, but the disturbing stench of the outside privy. The driver was named Ned Lein, and in case the authorities stopped him he had as his story the fact that he had been born and raised in La Crosse, and the fact that he still had blood relatives here. Although they had not laid eyes on him in more than a decade and would cringe at the thought of a visit from him. Most of them had consigned him safely to the dustbins of family legend at the time of the death of his mother, some ten years ago. Her death marked the last real tie Ned's La Crosse relatives were forced to maintain with Ned's troubled branch of the family.

Trouble had necessitated their removal from La Crosse, about twenty years ago, at the time Ned's father was sentenced to prison in Minnesota for having sex with the thirteen year old daughter of a fishing buddy from La Crescent. Theodore, the father, maintained stoutly that the oversexed wife of his buddy had made the whole story up when he, Theodore, refused to violate his oath of friendship and have sex with her. But there had been previous incidents, which came close to the same resolution, but had always been shoveled aside. Hilda, Ned's mother, moved Ned and his older sister Petra to a desolate sand farm, close to the center of Wisconsin, in the flat pine barrens not far from the sand-choked Wisconsin River.

Madeline was wearing the blue skirt that Ned liked to see her wear. Ned did not have a blue skirt like that in his collection and he wondered what his mother would look like wearing a blue skirt like that. He thought his mother was every bit as pretty as that girl he stared at, at least when she was a young girl she must have been. He was sure. He would think and see how it all looked. He was sure the Master would let him keep the clothes this time. Her body, well, that was not for Ned to worry about, at least not this time. But the clothes, at least the clothes would be his this time. He had put in a lot of work on this one.

Later that day:
(In the book section of the J.C. Penney's Store on 5th Avenue in downtown La Crosse)

The girl in the blue skirt hovered over a table of books consisting of large, over-sized art books, along with picture books or largely European travel books. The Master preferred Bernard to track the prey in social settings. Therefore, Bernard, in a seedy dark colored suit, huddled next to a paperback kiosk and idly thumbed *My Gun is Quick*. All the while he kept a wary eye on the girl in the blue skirt. Ned had stalked her by truck, but Ned did not blend well in the city. Bernard, despite his seedy, petty criminality, at least did not stink.

Later that day:

Bernard knew that he should not have let Ned drive the white colored Chevy they were transporting back to Madison. Sure as anything he will get stopped for something like speeding or driving like a jack ass. Which he does a lot. And sure enough, he gets stopped, fortunately one of the Master's servants came to rescue them at the Vernon County jail.

Chapter 3
Thursday, October 8, 1953
Viroqua, Wis.

Vernon County Court for traffic offenses was wending its way down a color speckled Autumn afternoon lane, in a leisurely, bored fashion, much like Cy Butt himself desired to be doing, as he gazed out the north windows of the courtroom. Cy was remembering other Autumn afternoons not so far from here, either lounging in hunting camps or visiting moonshine stills hidden at blind pig camps.

His eyes drifted over to the mural on the east side of the courtroom. He studied the pioneers emerging from a fairyland forest to gaze upon the shimmering surface of the Mississippi below them, at the far right side of the painted tableau. Father, mother, children accompany an anomalous herd of sheep. Two oxen pull a covered wagon. The mother and father, and an adolescent boy riding on one of the oxen ignore the observing American Indians who watch from the far left side of the painting. Only the smaller children see the Indians. These children are dressed like 19th century pampered aristocratic offspring of the East Coast. The older whites are more rough hewn. Cy pondered what message was being sent. He reflected upon the pioneer generation focused on the quest for the land, marching in lock step, often heedless of others, and how they were followed by later, more effete generations who looked off the path in the woods, looked at the wildflowers, and the Indians.

The quotes on the walls of the courtroom ranged from conservative, Edmund Burke: "Justice is itself the great standing policy of civil society; and eminent departure from it, under any circumstances lies under suspicion of being no policy at all", to imperial, Justinian: "Justice in the life and conduct of the state is possible only as first it resides in the hearts and souls of the citizens", to authoritarian, J.A. Froude: "Just laws are no restraint upon the freedom of the good for the good man desires nothing which a just law will interfere with." Cy had always thought it significant that the latter quote hovered over the jury box.

Cy was waiting for his client's case to be called up. He was here defending a pimply faced teenager, eighteen year old Tommy Torgerson, who had just started attending the University in Madison. The young scholar was charged with "excessive display of power and speed". This had become an all purpose coverall charge used by local police to curtail the cruising caravans of hot rodders that appeared every Saturday night, particularly warm Summer nights. The young man had been arrested one June night, months ago now, and Cy had used his time-honored tactic of asking for continuances and delays to annoy the judge and police to the extent that they would eventually throw the case out of court. And that was his plan today. It usually worked.

The county judge was a man very familiar to Cy, both in the court room and in the bar room. Judge Garfield Stensrude was a legend in the local Norwegian American community and a demigod in his hometown of Westby. Cy had often compared Stensrude to his gauzy childhood memories of his own illustrious grandfather, Col. C.M. Butt--himself the Vernon County judge for more than twenty years. Both men were capable of stirring crowds and particularly courtrooms with their mellow tones. Both men had the imprimatur of military service to help propel their careers down the dusty paths of Vernon County jurisprudence. Col. Butt had served in the Civil War and Stensrude had served in World War I in France. Cy measured himself against both men and found himself wanting. He had to be analytically honest, with himself, if not with others. He knew that he was no orator and could not evoke the flowery reverence heaped upon those men. Cy's military service had been in the Coast Guard during World War II, somewhat less electrifying in discourse than the sagas of the two judges. Nevertheless, he had not escaped approval by at least one of the judges. Cy recalled numerous times at the Viroqua Eagles Club or the VFW Club when Judge Stensrude, a bit in his cups, would level his long, graceful, bony index finger at the *bon vivant* and say: "Cy, if you weren't such a drunk, you could be sitting on the judge's bench right now. You have one of the finest legal minds I've ever encountered."

Indeed, unlike either his grandfather or Judge Stensrude, Cy Butt had made an absolute romance of books. He became as intoxicated by the smell of musty book bindings as he did by the taste of amber-colored whisky--although few of his bar room associates would believe that notion. As a result of this, lonely research was the great forte of his legal career and intellectual life. And the book stacks of Madison were like a great cave system where he found refuge and quietly healed old wounds when he did not want to use drink as an anodyne.

Cy spent hour after day, day after decade in the libraries of the University of Wisconsin, Madison, and of the City of Madison, and of the State Government of Wisconsin--an archipelago of libraries scattered in several dozen hissing steam heated nooks as well as drafty, cavernous study halls of the City between the Two Lakes. And Cy was never happier than when he bent his wiry form into a pretzel and sat in any book lined paradise. This was when he was not trolling the bars of Madison for information, and good times. He had unearthed long forgotten Madison city ordinances and waved them jauntily in the faces of authorities. One example was the one which gave citizens in public a right to wear side arms in visible holsters. He marched up State Street one afternoon with such a gun and holster strapped on the outside of his threadbare, brown suit coat. Sure enough, after a couple of blocks he was arrested by a Madison policeman, and a weeklong controversy raged in city hall which resulted in the dismissal of all charges and the quiet repeal of the ordinance.

Cy enjoyed these direct confrontations with the powers that be. However, today his strategy was to retreat, to sidestep the issue like a cautious cat, and come back on another occasion when the powers that be were too burdened with actual, dangerous crimes to prosecute the misdemeanors. His client, Tommy Torgerson, the young lad sitting in the row ahead of him, was not dangerous to society. Nor even was the insurance agent from Green Bay, four hours away from Vernon County (as he kept pointing out), who just now was vigorously contesting his ticket for driving through a stop sign with "a rolling stop". Terms such as "speed trap" were being tossed around by this man, who was acting as his own attorney. A perfect example, Cy thought, of the old aphorism: "a man who acts as his own lawyer has a fool for a client". Cy would have cautioned him to calm down, be respectful, bring the facts to the surface not emotions.

Cy was certain that the outraged salesman from Green Bay was about to get the book forcefully hurled at him by the visibly impatient Judge Stensrude, who now hunched his tall, burly, black-robed form over the surface of his bench like a large buzzard contemplating a meal. Not pretty, thought Cy.

To lighten his mood Cy turned his eyes secretly to Gwen Torgerson, the mother of his young client. Two decades ago she had been Cy's lover. Cy liked to fantasize that the boy himself was his own son, but he knew full well that the math just did not add up. The woman was now a ruddy complexioned farmwife with flaring Norwegian cheekbones and still pouting lips, and a still shapely form. Cy recalled necking with her on Sunday evenings on the bus returning to Madison, where she was trying to construct a nursing career. Her overbearing father would later smash that career, her hopes, and Cy's hopes to splinters like a wrathful tornado. But on those blissful nights in the early 1930s, Cy smooched with the young farm girl, fragrant of her perfume and her father's cows. This woman now sat in the row ahead of Cy, along with her stolid Norwegian farmer husband and the eighteen year old defendant. Cy watched the family trio whisper quietly.

"But your honor! I protest!" screamed the insurance salesman as the judge rendered his decision and pronounced his sentence of $100.

"Any more talk like that sir and I'll fine you for contempt of court! Might I also add that a court is not unlike a church...." Judge Stensrude intoned.

Here we go, thought Cy, with an inward grin-- careful to make sure that Stensrude saw no smirk or other expression of levity on his face.

"There are millions of men and women toiling under the taskmasters of tyranny worldwide who would pay their eye teeth to have a chance to appear in a courtroom such as this. Instead their governments render decisions at the point of guns and the crack of whips. We have fought numerous wars to protect these rights for our citizens, sir, and--

"But your honor, I must object--" whined the salesman.

Wrong move thought Cy.

"Sir, one more such interruption I will not only fine you but jail you next door. " The judge's head made a contemptuous jerk to the left, toward the large window through which the county jail could be viewed. "Now I have rendered my decision and if you feel you have grounds for appeal please try to press your case through conventional legal means and hire yourself a lawyer. Next case!"

And crack went the judge's gavel. The bailiff politely but firmly urged the man toward the exit. For just a moment it seemed like he might launch into a new complaint, but finally he shrugged his shoulders and walked through the little gate separating the courtroom seating area from the judge and lawyer's area.

Whew thought Cy. Cy was glad that his was not the next case. Never good to plead a case in front of a judge already riled up by the previous one.

Cy began to turn his attention to the young Assistant District Attorney. Malcolm Prentiss was a recent transplant from Illinois. He had been hired by the aging District Attorney, Ole Nordsgarden, on a recommendation from a former law partner--so Cy had heard. The law partner now worked for an oil company out of an enormous suite of offices in downtown Chicago. Cy was certain that the young man was looked upon by Nordsgarden as the rising star that Nordsgarden himself could have been if he had joined his erstwhile partner in Chicago, years ago.

Young Mr. Prentiss now turned his gaze to a trio of figures Cy had hitherto ignored. This was a simple speeding charge that took place in the Village of La Farge three days ago. Three men sat in the front row, far over on the right side, almost directly under the authoritarian quote from J.A. Froude. One man, clearly the lawyer, was a pudgy faced, blond haired man of indeterminate age, although he was clearly not young. He wore a finely tailored suit and carried an immaculate leather briefcase. Small wire rimmed glasses sat upon his nose. A strangely unnerving perpetual smile seemed to be chiseled onto the man's face. He sat between two rather contrasting figures.

One was evidently a late middle aged farmer of some sort, although he gave a vague impression of a certain mental disarray in his unshaven face and fearful, even wild look. He was dressed in a denim jacket with blue jeans and blue work shirt. The other man was much younger than his two companions. This short, weasel-faced man was dressed in a gaudy, plaid, sports coat, white shirt, flowered tie, and black pants. This man, while superficially well-dressed, gave the impression of wearing clothes that he had slept in. He also resembled some kind of low level gangster.

Much to the surprise of Cy Butt, and apparently to the surprise of the judge and the Sheriff--sharp featured Warren Mars who sat directly behind the prosecution table--Assistant District Attorney Prentiss launched into a long, friendly conversation with the blond haired defense lawyer. This lawyer was from La Crosse. The charge was a fairly minor traffic violation--speeding. While the defendants did not dispute the charge, for some reason, their lawyer was determined to have the charge totally dismissed. The Sheriff was soon drawn into this discussion which was beginning to annoy the judge to such an extent that he was making impatient sighing and coughing noises. The Sheriff was clearly upset about the conversation between Prentiss and the blond haired lawyer. He was still whispering, in a loud, choppy, stage whisper. Finally, the judge could wait no longer:

"Mr. Prentiss, the court is ready for you to present the next case. It is the people versus Ned Lein--

"Your honor!" said Prentiss suddenly, an interruption equally as annoying to the judge as the interruptions of the Green Bay insurance salesman.

"Your honor, may I approach the bench." said Prentiss, looking back at the blond haired lawyer with an obsequious expression on his face.

"You may, Mr. Prentiss." growled Judge Stensrude, who then made a dark, knowing scowl in the direction of Sheriff Mars. Prentiss then approached the bench and what ensued was another whispered conversation. From time to time, the judge would say something like:

"I don't see the point"

And Prentiss could be heard saying: "It's such a minor charge your honor."

"Very well, Mr. Prentiss. It is your decision to make-- for the people." said Judge Stensrude, giving a quick assessing look over at the farmer and gangster. He then turned away in disgust. The judge intoned, words dripping with sarcasm. "The charges are withdrawn. Case dismissed." he said, banging his gravel with a look of sheer contempt aimed at the Assistant District Attorney. The judge now looked mischievously in the direction of Cy Butt as he said:

"Next case!"

And the Assistant District Attorney began reading the litany of noise and speed charges against the young man. The judge broke Prentiss off with a sudden announcement:

"It's such a minor charge." the judge said, now directly looking at the Assistant District Attorney. "Case dismissed! Court adjourned!" A decisive rap of the gavel echoed through the high ceiling courtroom.

"Your honor!!!" shouted the Assistant District Attorney and the Sheriff at the same time as they both converged upon the judge's bench. Cy exchanged quick looks with the judge--who actually seemed to wink at him before he turned sternly to his dissatisfied associates.

Cy happily shook hands with his young client, then felt his hands crushed by the ham-sized, rough hewn hands of Thomas Sr., his client's gruff-mannered, but noble father, and finally gently caressed the farm work-hardened, small, gentle hands of his client's mother, Gwen. He exchanged a quick look with her, nodded with atypical discomfort and silence as the father promised to get a check in the mail the very next day. Then Cy sauntered out of the courtroom into the hallway--his battered, bulging leather brief case carried by his right hand, his crumpled wide brimmed hat on his head. He could still hear the happy family chatter of his young client and the parents in the courtroom. He realized that a tear was etching itself across the surface of his right eye. Quickly he dispatched the index finger and the palm of his left hand to assuage that emotion. He stood beside a floor to ceiling window and to get his mind off his long-lost-love he watched the blond lawyer from La Crosse and the two mysterious clients get into a cream-colored Packard parked on maple-cloaked Decker Street.

Suddenly, he realized somebody was coming up behind him. Fearful that it was his young client, and the parental unit, he resisted turning around. Then he heard a familiar voice, and he turned and saw Philio DeGarmo.

"Cy, can we have a word?" asked Philio "Let's go outside on the yard."

By the time the two men had reached the large, tree-dotted yard of the Vernon County courthouse, the crème-colored Packard was a distant blur, far down

Decker Street, turning left onto Highway 14 for its return to La Crosse. Philio noticed Cy watching the car.

"That is what I want to talk with you about, Cy. There is something funny about that lawyer, and his two clients." said Philio. "However, except for today's traffic charge----"

"--Which was thrown out of court incidentally." said Cy.

"What?" asked Philio incredulously. "Why?"

Cy described the odd turn of events today in the courtroom.

"Then Grover must be on to something." said Philio.

"What do you mean?" asked Cy.

"Grover has been tracking that lawyer for some time. He never seems to break the law, but he comes perilously close. He also has some very powerful friends. And some exceedingly foul friends, witness today. A lot of suspicious European money. So, an overt investigation of him is risky. It could be considered to be harassment, but nevertheless he bears watching. So we need an unconventional researcher." said Philio,

"And that means me." said Cy, with a conspiratorial grin.

"Exactly" said Philio.

The two men climbed into Philio's two passenger Nash. Philio drove Cy over to the Hotel Fortney, where Cy kept a room while in Viroqua. Upstairs, in Cy's cramped third floor corner room overlooking Viroqua's Main Street, Philio opened up a box which contained an experimental listening device from Attorney General Townsend. He briefed Cy on the operation of the machine and told him to focus on the two men the lawyer defended in court as much as the lawyer. One of them, Bernard, was a paroled ex-convict from the central part of the state. The other, Ned Lein, was a complete mystery. He was a late middle-aged bachelor farmer also from central Wisconsin. He had no criminal history at all. Why the two of them were suddenly chumming around was unknown.

"In Madison, we believe that these two might somehow be linked to various car thefts. That was why it was interesting that one of them was charged here in court on a traffic offense. The police originally thought the car they were driving then was stolen, but a search of the motor vehicle records turned up nothing. Supposedly."

"What do you mean supposedly?" asked Cy.

"There seems to be an unseen hand protecting these two. Case in point--your assistant D.A. dropping the case, over the objections of the Sheriff. We have been looking into Mr. Prentiss for a number of reasons." said Philio, who gave Cy a knowing look.

Cy had a couple of quick drinks from his hip flask. Philio, as was his wont, refused Cy's offer to indulge. In a bit, the two men descended the narrow stairway of the ancient brick hotel and climbed into Philio's tiny car. Off they went to La Crosse, where Cy checked into the Hotel Stoddard to begin his research. Philio returned to Madison immediately.

Chapter 4
Friday, October 9, 1953
La Crosse, Wis.

Cy Butt sat in a tree next to a window of a small, unlicensed bar across the river from La Crosse. The establishment, Pete's Bait Shop, did actually sell bait in a front room. The greater part of the rambling, wood-frame building--resting upon pilings pounded into the muck of the river bed--was a 'private club'. On the first floor, it consisted of a fish and bait shop in the front, and a bar in the rear. It had various single rooms upstairs. Signs behind the back bar indicated that these rooms were for rent by the day, week, or month. This was one Wisconsin bar that Cy Butt avoided, although he had drunk here. Tonight, he was listening to the bar. Cy did not want to be even seen here tonight. He had spent the day following two men around La Crosse. They were definitely up to something, but he could make no sense of pointless visits to department stores and drives around the streets of La Crosse. So, he was hidden in a tree with the high powered eaves dropping instrument given to him by Philio. He was trying to sift through of the jumble of conversations in the bar room:

"That fish was as long as my arm---"

"Gimme a beer and a shot"

"I got a car here, stole it from---"

"Big deal, I've caught bigger fish"

"So I told my boss, take this job and---"

"The Master says he's interested in the fifteen year old--"

"And gimme a hamburger too."

"It's not like there is only one machine shop in this town."

"All I want is her clothes."

"Well, you wanta hear about big fish?..."

"No, not a Miller, a Schlitz..."

"A guy has to be drunk to run lathe."

"Gimme a pack of Lucky Strikes"

"..before the end of the month, a weekend..."

"I worked once down at the lock and dam at Ferryville"

"Ya, ya, laxative Schlitz, right, very funny."

"There's catfish as big as a cow there behind the dams."

"The Master wants her alive to start with, after that who cares--"

Cy found this task as frustrating as listening to far off radio stations in the middle of the night. And indeed, that is really what he was doing, except the stations were a few feet away, through a partly opened window. The window was so dirty he could not clearly make out faces. Although he had about decided the voices he was most interested in came from a small, weasely-looking man, in a tacky coat and tie, and a tall gaunt figure in a farmer's cap. They were apart from the rest of the crowd. Not far from the window. Cy was glad the eavesdropping machine had headphones, otherwise the two men could have probably overhead their own words.

Suddenly, the radio of a barge somewhere out on the fog covered river blasted its interference into both of Cy's eardrums. He could not help crying out in pain, and as he jerked he accidentally pulled the earphone loose.

"We snatch her when she's alone...What's that?...that?...that?"

"What's what?"

"Don't you hear it?..it?...it?...it?"

"I hear you sittin' here."

"But I hear myself. Outside...side...side."

The weasely man rose and walked directly to the partly opened window. Cy was so stunned and shocked he lost his grip and fell down the trunk of the tree. He could feel his battered, vaguely Vitalis-smelling hat (with sewn in label: Felix's Clothing Store--Viroqua, Wis., upon which the words: "Cy Butt" were scribbled in indelible ink) catch on a tree branch as he fell. He didn't dare grab for it because he was hanging onto the listening device. He still held the device as he hit the surface of the water. He hadn't realized that he retained such a natural ability to swim, particularly after having imbibed a few whiskeys prior to his sojourn up the tree. Perhaps it was some kind of innate psychological defense mechanism. A self preservation thing built into his primate wiring. After all, he knew his mental condition on that particular night was off-kilter, as he would have an hallucination of being carried to shore by a giant catfish. He remembered that for years.

Chapter 5
Saturday, October 10, 1953
Madison, Wis.

P hilio heard the taxi stop outside his College Heights rooming house around midnight, just as he began to drift off to sleep. Then he heard the beginning of the argument. The subject seemed to be a taxi bill, and flashing its way throughout the dialogue on the fog-enshrouded, twisting, hillside streets was the rasping voice of Cy Butt. Philio put on his pants, left his room, and descended to the street to see what Cy was involved in this time. He suspected that it might have something to do with the mission Attorney General Grover W. Townsend had sent Cy Butt to pursue in La Crosse.

Philio knew that sleeping students and faculty were being roused from their warm beds by this noise, so he resolved to bring things to an end whatever it took. It took a ten dollar bill.

"That is highway robbery!" screamed Cy. His loudest retort so far. His words echoing against the vine-covered walls of turn of the century academic villas built upon the hill overlooking Camp Randall stadium.

"Listen old man, I won't find any return run up in this nowhere neighborhood. I'm gonna have to run empty all the way back to the square or University Avenue just to find another fare. That costs money. You gonna pay or am I gonna call the cops?"

"Show him your badge Philio, that will shut him up." snickered Cy.

"Pipe down Cy." Philio said , reaching into his pants for his billfold, fishing out a ten dollar bill. "What are you doing here at this time of night? Let's get off the street."

They went upstairs to Philio's small apartment, where they sat facing each other at the table in the kitchenette.

"What are you doing here Cy?" asked Philio. "Are you on some kind of bender? You don't really look drunk. Did you find out something about those two men?"

"I'm sober as the proverbial judge Philio. And I never wished more to be drunk. At least then I could forget what I have just learned about my home state." Cy said, leveling an oddly intense stare at Philio.

"What on Earth are you talking about Cy?" Philio wondered what Cy could have unearthed in La Crosse.

"I've found out about a crime, a coming crime, an abduction at the very least, of some young girl, maybe, from somewhere." Cy rambled. Finally, he ended by staring out the window at the now quiet and vacant street, as if he were watching for somebody to come after him.

"Are the two men you saw in Vernon County Court doing this?" asked Philio.

"Yes, but I don't know why." answered Cy.

"Well, these sex criminals don't need any reason. They are just animals." said Philio firmly.

"This is more than a sex crime, although I'm sure that sex is involved somehow. This is about some kind of group." said Cy.

"A group of sex criminals?" asked Philio.

"Yes,..and no. There is more than sex. There must be." said Cy.

"How did you find all this out?" asked Philio.

Cy narrated his misadventure shinnied up a tree wedged between Pete's Bait Shop and the Mississippi River, of eavesdropping upon the conversation between Ned and Bernard, and of finally falling into the river. He did not mention his hallucination of being carried to safety on a sandbar by a giant catfish.

After a long moment of silence while he turned Cy's extraordinary recitation over and over in his mind Philio finally asked: "Shall I make some coffee then, Cy?"

"Yes, please do." said Cy. Pulling his hip flask out of his inside coat pocket.

Well, thought Philio. That is more like it.

Finally, sleep overcame both of them. Philio went back to bed and Cy bunked on the couch in Philio's book-strewn living room.

The next morning, Philio drove Cy home. Cy Butt lived in a small apartment off Langdon Street. Philio drove back to College Heights. Meanwhile, Cy walked up to his second floor apartment, unlocked the door, turned on the light, and there on the hallway table, next to the phone, was that wet, vaguely Vitalis-smelling hat he had lost in that tree along the Mississippi River in La Crosse.

Chapter 6
Saturday, October 10, 1953
La Crosse, Wis.

A s Cy and Philio prepared for their morning in Madison, Madeline Marley and her family were beginning a calm, ordinary Saturday morning. Mom, Eleanor Marley, was in the kitchen frying up bacon and eggs as she did every morning. Pop, or Prof. Norman Marley was sitting at the kitchen table reading the morning paper. Chip, or Charles, was at the table too, as was Kitten, or Madeline.

Yes, it was the Marleys. The daily family drama, staring an American family living on the suburban frontier. Madeline and her brother had really initiated the use of the radio soap opera style nicknames--as heard on "One Man's Family", "Vic and Sade", and other radio programs the family enjoyed together. Probably her younger brother had started the joke. But all the rest of them had joined in because it was funny and made them feel their bond as a family. And they were a bonded, united family. It showed, and outsiders could see it. That alone made Madeline an appealing target for evil.

Madeline had decided to use this morning's breakfast time to spring her new proposal to become a babysitter. A lot of her friends at school had already taken up this lucrative practice, and while she had no particular goal for which to save money (except that trip to Paris she had long since resolved to take someday) she could still use the money for movies, clothes, and sodas at the lunch counter at the downtown *Grant's* department store on 5th Avenue.

"Say, Pop..." Madeline began, using that tentative, anticipatory tone she had learned to use while speaking with her father if she was making a proposal she wanted him to seriously consider.

"Yes, Kitten." Pop replied, partly lowering his paper, and looking at Kitten, with a smile.

"Pop, what would you think about it if I put up a small sign at church asking for babysitting jobs?" Kitten spilled it all out, breathlessly.

Mom and Chip watched the other two, silently.

Pop looked over at Mom, inquiringly.

Mom nodded with a firm compressed smile on her lips, then said:

"Well, Norm. She is a very responsible girl. I was babysitting myself when I was her age."

Pop nodded, smiled, and said:

"Ok, kitten, I think I have a job for you already." Pop looked over at Mom. "young Professor Magnussen wants to thank me for help in his article on the Brontes. He asked if we might be interested in going out to eat after the game on October 24th. He asked me if I knew about a babysitter." Pop looked over at Kitten.

Madeline jumped up, sprang around the table and gave her father a big hug.

"Oh, thank you Poppie!!!" she cried.

"Pops, if Maddie can baby-sit, can I get a 22 rifle?." asked young Chip.

"Not for another year, Chip." Pop said firmly.

"Ah, jeez, Pop." said Chip.

And breakfast went on with no further important developments.

Chapter 7
Monday, October 12, 1953
Madison, Wis.

C y had a great fondness for the funeral firm of Milton and Drydens. They were the ones who buried little Bonnie DiMarco in Resurrection Cemetery on Madison's then just a'borning west side.

Cy Butt had first stumbled across her grave one day in the late 1940s, in one of his periodic cemetery walks. Her youth, and the tragic murder that carried her to that grave both touched Cy to the depths of his soul. Cy ever despised anyone who would hurt children. From his own childhood, he had felt this way.

Milton and Drydens Funeral Home had always been one of Cy's favorite hangouts. Especially if he had a snoot full and needed a quiet place to just sit and maybe gossip. Moreover, when he found out that Milton and Drydens had buried Bonnie DiMarco, Cy had begun pumping his sources there for information on that long remembered tragedy. Cy also loved the ornate stone carved gargoyles perched upon the pediments of Milton and Drydens Funeral Home on University Avenue. Charlie Riemer was a long time employee of the firm. Moreover, he came from, if not Viroqua, then the nearby Kickapoo Valley, Blissville, to be exact. He was sort of homefolk, and Cy was not averse to using such a connection to glean information from someone if his need be. This was what he was doing on this particular day as he wandered into the open garage door of the funeral home, in search of Charlie.

Meanwhile, Cy had been followed to the Milton and Drydens Funeral Home by Bernard, the short, weasel-faced man who had appeared in the Vernon County court room, this time in a dingy dark suit. He slipped into the open garage door as Butt entered the building. He slid with the silence of a rodent next to the long, black Cadillac hearse in the first bay. He cautiously approached the open door Cy had entered. Down a long hallway he saw Butt open a door and reveal a brightly lit room, from which gushed the sound of running water and an incessant radio. Butt held the door open, gossiping to a man inside. Bernard could just make out a short, fat, balding man, who was talking out of one side of his mouth and holding and smoking a cigarette with the other side. What really attracted Bernard's attention was the female corpse on a long table in front of the smoking fat man. The fat man appeared to be holding some sort of long, sharp, pointed tube in his hand as he gestured to Cy. The two men appeared to be picking up a conversation which had begun perhaps days ago. Bernard watched in fascination as the fat man speared the sharp instrument into the woman's body and withdrew fluids.

The fat man said as he worked:

"No, Cy, I don't think there ever was much of an autopsy."

"How could they not do an autopsy? It was the biggest murder in the history of the city"

"Well don't ask me. I don't run Madison and I sure as hell didn't run it in 1918."

The phone rang. The fat man talked on it rapidly, jotting down information as he asked questions and listened. Finally he said "Thanks" Hung up and said to Cy: "Come on, Cy we gotta go. You can help me pick up a body."

"Oh, jeez Charlie. Where do we have to go?"

"Just St. Mary's Hospital. It's practically next door."

"More like 20 blocks.

"Either way. It's closer than Viroqua! Why don't you help out an old Kickapogian to pay for all that info you get out of me."

"Okay. What rig are we taking?"

"Jump in that Cadillac right near the door."

Bernard made a dive for the nearby hearse. He opened a side door, and spied a compartment for a spare tire, a collapsible casket carrier called a church truck, flower stands, and other items. Bernard managed to wedge his scrawny form into the compartment. Cy and Charlie loaded a cot over Bernard and got into the front of the hearse. They backed out of the garage and began the journey to St. Mary's Hospital. Hindered by the sound of the tires sloshing through puddles in the streets, Bernard listened: "You know, Cy, I hate what they are doing to this goddamn town. I gotta good mind to quit here and go back home. I could get a job in Viroqua."

"What don't you like about Madison?"

"Well, it's the damned university and the city. Conspiring together to drive out all the cheap housing. They say they are going to build high rise dorms. Like in that movie, "Metropolis", with everybody in big high buildings and four-lane highways between. You think that will ever come to Madison, Cy?"

"Not in my lifetime, nor yours. But maybe sometime down the line. A century maybe."

"Well here we are driving through the Greenbush neighborhood, the poor Italian and foreign digs, and they say some big shots are going to buy up all these little houses and bulldoze 'em."

"No kidding? Where you hear that?"

"I heard it. And it was from a guy pretty-well tied in over at city hall"

"Why you taking Park Street?"

"Because it's the best way to St. Mary's that's why."

"No it isn't. Bassett Street would be better."

"Not from Milton and Dryden it ain't. Maybe from some of your favorite bars it is."

Cy appeared to have no audible answer to this remark. Bernard could hear Cy moving around a bit on his seat. Then he heard Charlie say: "Don't mind if I do Cy."

Then they both made drinking noises, and Charlie at least made something like gasping noises: "That's pretty good stuff Cy. That didn't come from no factory did it?"

"Not any factory that pays taxes. It came from up north. From an old guy I know up around Hurley."

"Where'd you get this hip flask?"

"Frank Lloyd Wright gave it to me."

"Bull--

"I mean it."

"You probably do."

"Do you ever get scared of death, Charlie?"

"I can't say that I do, Cy"

"Do you think seeing so much death has left any scars?"

"On me?"

"Well, there ain't anybody else here is there?" (cackles)

"I think it has. I know it has. Bonnie DiMarco for one, that did."

"How old were you then?"

"About eighteen. I had just started working at Milton and Drydens Funeral Parlor. Later on I went to mortuary school. I was just a flunky then. Maybe not more than that now (He laughed sardonically).

"The DiMarco house was right around here someplace wasn't it?"

"Yes. Over on S. Francis St. I'll go the long way and swing past the block. We'll go down Regent and you can look down Francis. I don't want to take the hearse on them narrow streets unless I have to ." (Sardonic laughter.) "Give me another pull of that stuff. Fine"

"Hey, easy up. I've got to get through the rest of the day on that."

"Sure, right. Tell me another one. Like you can't get a free drink anywhere in the City of Madison."

"Well, that is a point for contention. That's the street isn't it?"

"Yes, right up there. (long pause) I was over at the funeral home when the cops brought her in."

"And you say they did no autopsy?"

"No, I didn't say that. I said they didn't do much of

an autopsy. And this town is full of doctors and professors. They opened her up, took some samples, took some photos. There were reporters all over the place. The police brought in some old quack from the south side to do it. Why they didn't get somebody from the medical school is beyond me. I remember the quack had some young guy with him."

"Who was the quack? Who was the young guy?"

"The quack was old man Carstairs, who got arrested in the 30s for doing abortions. You remember?"

(Cy coughed) "Yes I remember him."

"The young guy was supposed to be some student from Europe. A creepy guy.

"Where was he from in Europe? France? Germany?"

"I don't know. Maybe both. Or maybe he was American but of European parents. I don't know. But I've seen him other times."

"What other times?"

"Other murders. And we've had our share of them. We don't bury the carriage crowd, as you know."

"Yes, I know. But this young guy--"

"Well, I don't remember much. It's funny. I can remember the guy unless I try to think about him. But anyway, I remember he always showed up with doctors or cops. And then usually not the best type of them either. If you know what I mean. People who later on get brought up for charges. And he always showed up at murder investigations. I've seen him maybe three times since 1918. And another weird thing--I have gotten older, but he has stayed the same. He's a hefty man, bald, he was then in 1918. Small beard. But the last time I saw him--late 40s, I guess, he looked like he hadn't aged a bit. And look at me, fatter, wrinkled, missing teeth. But I'm still the same person. Isn't that amazing? Even the same since I was a kid. That's amazing too."

"I'm sure it is, but--"

"In fact, I don't think my real soul and essence..."

"Oh, brother..."

"No, I mean it Cy. Listen. You know I went to the funeral of the first guy ever born in this town? Did I ever tell you?"

"No, I guess not."

"His name was Madison. James Madison Stoner. He was born in a shack somewhere a block or so off the Capitol Square. Except then it was a big forest. Just a cabin or two here and there. In the 1830s sometime. But they were building Madison right then. And they said they had to name this kid after Madison. And they did. He died out on the poor farm near Verona about 1921. Old Emil Frautschi bought him a grave lot over in Forest Hill cemetery. I was working in their embalming room then. We all stood around the grave, I remember it was Armistice Day, 1921. That made it somehow sadder. And I'm still the kid I was then. And I bet the guy we buried felt like he was the same guy out on the poor farm as he was as a kid growing up in the forests that became Madison."

Cy shouted a sort of command to Charlie as the vehicle backed up: "Clear on this side Charlie!"

And both men left the vehicle and took with them the body cot which had been riding on floor of the back of the hearse, above the compartment holding Bernard, the spare tire, et. al. Bernard took this as his opportunity to slip out of the car and hot foot it down the street.

Chapter 8
Tuesday, October 13, 1953
South of Cassville, Wis.,
on banks of Mississippi River

A ninety-eight-year-old African-American man, Enoch Clover, was sitting on the eastern bank of the Mississippi River, in a secluded, willow-enshrouded lagoon. He was bald, his face almost a perfect oval, his shiny black scalp totally bare in a gentle round curve. The late afternoon sun had begun its descent into the blue colored Iowa hills, far across the shimmering water. The trees had long since entered their Fall color season. However, the raucous reds and shocking crimsons were now giving way to the gentle yellows, and browns. Many trees were now bare. The sunlight was a sparkling sheen on the flat, still surface of the great, green river. It was so bright in his eyes that Enoch carefully kept an overhang of willow trees between the river and himself. There was another reason Enoch sat in this sheltered cove. He held his fishing pole with both hands, kneeling on the ground Indian-style, the end of the pole resting between his legs, in the sandy bank of the river. He watched the surface of the river intently.

Enoch had persuaded his friend Ken Starky, a publisher and book store owner in nearby Platteville, to drive him over to the river. Enoch lived in the back of Ken's store in exchange for custodial services. Ken did not enjoy fishing, and as Enoch had hoped, Ken was taking this time to visit friends in nearby Beetown. He would return in a couple of hours to pick up Enoch, and they both would return to Platteville and the cozy bookstore where they both lived. Enoch had been counting on things to work out that way, because he did not want Ken or anybody else around to see what was about to happen.

The dark, green surface of the water began to show a disturbance. A bubbling came up from deep below. Gradually, something began to show itself. An enormous, dull, blade-shaped form surfaced and moved slowly toward Enoch from its location still far out in the river. Spikes or feelers could be seen along this blade. Now the blade could be seen to be set on the top of a large round shape. And now the large round shape could be seen to have a face, with two eyes and a mouth--looking directly at Enoch, who continued to sit calmly on the river bank. However, he reeled in his fishing line and put his fishing pole aside.

A large body now emerged from beneath the face--a body that looked very much like a fish standing on end. The blade was a sort of fin going from its face, over its head and down its back. The creature approached Enoch who sat amidst a grove of willow trees. It got to about ten feet away from the bank. The lower part of its body remained in the water. Its mouth formed a sort of smile and it said:

"Greetings Enoch."

"Greetings Nommo." said Enoch.

The branches of the willow trees formed a tent over the water in which the Nommo stood. The creature could only be seen from Enoch's direction.

"You have done well, Enoch, with the knowledge we have given you. Just as your ancestors did well with the knowledge that we gave them. Your spirit will soon depart from this world and you will soon join your ancestors in another world."

"Thank you Nommo. I have always tried to use the knowledge you gave me wisely." said Enoch.

The Creature said: "But you have one last task, Enoch. There is an evil man who is in contact with creatures who come from the stars like Ogo, and like the other Nommos and myself. They are reptiles who descended from heaven sticking to Ogo's bloody placenta. They are the *brankamaza* and the *kaka bamagommolo*. Some of them have burrowed into the earth awaiting the time to emerge and that is now. Some of these creatures are small, they have big heads, discolored bodies, and frail limbs, and they live in holes in the Earth. Some of them are large and green. These creatures are highly populous in the Earth's interior. Ogo and the snakes met in space on the way to Earth and when the star Sirius comes they will meet each other again. These beings are imperfect and now they have become allied with evil men. Good men have to fight them. ."

"What do you want me to do Nommo? I am old and weak. And you yourself have said I am going to die soon." pleaded Enoch.

"The only thing you can do Enoch is to make sure that other humans know something about this."

"How can I do this without telling them about you? You've always wanted me to keep you secret." said Enoch.

"In this case you can tell them about me. They won't believe you anyway. They will think your mind is damaged by the sickness inside of you. But we know that is not true, Enoch."

"Yes, we do Nommo. Nommo, why don't you, with the great knowledge you have, defeat this evil man, and the creatures who help him.

"Enoch, my child, I have told you before. We cannot do anything for you that you cannot do yourselves. We are both creations of God, Amma. The snake creatures are creatures of Amma, God. Just as Ogo, just as you, me, everyone, and we all have our own paths. Tell your friend Ken about me, about the snake people who are working with evil men, and above all tell them that these creatures plan to kidnap and sacrifice a pure virgin. Tell them that they have tunnels under the Earth, which they do. Tell them that a particularly evil man is using them and being used by them to achieve power, using the knowledge about Sirius that we Nommos gave to you Dogon people from God, Amma." said the Nommo.

Chapter 9
Wednesday, Oct. 14, 1953
Madison, Wis.

"**D**id you gentlemen realize?..." Cy paused for a sip on the whiskey and water he had been dallying with, "that you can trace the birth of Madison in a way you can't with most cities. What day did London begin? Or Paris, or Chicago? Nobody knows. But in the case of Madison there was a specific day when the sawing and hammering got started. That day was June 7, 1837. That was the day the crew arrived to start building the State Capitol building which the Wisconsin Territorial Council had voted to build a few months earlier in November of 1836. That vote had been taken in Belmont, a place not much bigger now than it was then, a few hundred souls, but at least it continues to be, which is more than you can say for Helena, which doesn't exist at all really, except as a few fishing shacks. But even that condition is better than life as a paper city--like Wisconsinapolis. However, in Nov. of 1836, Madison itself was nothing more than a paper city. A city of dreams in the mind of Judge James Doty. All these places I've mentioned were nominees. Helena, Belmont, Wisconsinapolis, Madison, but also Fond du Lac, Dubuque, Portage, Milwaukee,

Racine, Mineral Point, Platteville, Astor, Cassville, Belleville, Koshkenong, Peru and Wisconsin City. I can't remember which ones were real and which ones were not."

Cy paused for another drink and to eye his crowd. Red, the bartender, and old Siera, the Italian stone cutter who spent his time coughing up his lungs, here and in his tiny Greenbush apartment. Both Red and Siera seemed languidly bored, tolerant, maybe even desirous of hearing another installment. So Cy obliged:

"The man who built the State Capitol was a slaver from Illinois named James Morrison. He kept at least two female slaves with him in Madison during the construction of the capitol building and some time thereafter. This was along with a wife, so I figure they were mostly household servants. But they were still slaves. It was legal to keep them in Wisconsin Territory if you came in from some other state, and a lot of people did. You just couldn't buy them here. Things would change after this place became a state, and an anti-slavery one at that, but that hadn't happened yet, and wouldn't for another twelve years. This place was developing its character. Southerners were coming up into the Lead District. That was a big industry then. The lead over at Galena and Platteville was a key strategic asset. Bullets could be made out of it. Just like uranium out west today."

Cy could see Siera and Red thinking that one over.

"Easterners were coming in on the Great Lakes, down the Erie Canal. People from New York. These were people who were radicals and believed in stuff like Loco-Focoism. Ever heard of that?"

Both men shook their heads.

"It was an early form of radical Democrat. People to the left of Andy Jackson and Martin Van Buren. They mostly lived in New York City and believed in stuff like removing the property ownership requirement for voting, paving the streets, and other radical nonsense. Meanwhile, the Southerners over in the Lead District were pretty conservative. A lot of them were slavers, included big wheeler-dealers like Gov. Henry Dodge, who had his own little Fort Dodge at Dodgeville. And James Morrison. Who had mines over at Blue Mounds. Morrison also had pigs penned up in the basement of the state capitol here in Madison when he was building it. He even kept them there after the legislature had started meeting in the unfinished building. And he kept the slaves down there, too, among the pigs. He had built the whole place with green lumber, so all the boards shrunk horribly when the building was closed up for the winter and exposed to the wood stoves. The floor of the assembly chamber developed cracks between the floorboards, and Morrison's pigs down in the basement could be observed in their usually peaceful activities. But they say that assembly members would stick long poles down through the floor and rile up the pigs below to drown out the voices of opposition speakers! Haha! And all the while the slaves standing silently among the pigs look up at the legislature. A veritable tableau of the repressed reality of politics in the Ante-Bellum Era!! Hahaha!!!" Cy laughed joyously at the conclusion of his tale.

And everybody laughed at this great tale, which was worth the telling. Each and every time. And with a flourish, Cy finished off the last of his drink and headed for the restroom.

Red watched Cy leave the room, and then he wiped up an invisible stain on the bar before he turned to the only other customer in the place--this time at 2:30 P.M. Evidently, everybody was off somewhere else, and that's what Red said to the other customer--Italian stone cutter Siera, who lived in the nearby Greenbush neighborhood:

"Everybody else has got something else to do this afternoon except you, me, and him."

"It's not good to drink this time of the day." said the old man, censoriously.

"Oh yes." said Red laughing, with undisguised irony. "You're right. It's not really good to drink anytime." Red continued, with a smile. And then he paused, waiting for Siera.

"Now, take that man who was just in here....." Siera continued, pausing.

"Cy Butt...?" asked Red, on cue. Encouragingly.

"Yes," said Siera, studying Red's thin face before he continued. "I've known that man for almost thirty years. He was a young student here in the 20s, and the bootleggers, and the thirties and the Commies and the Nazis, and the war, and everything else, and he's been here that whole time." Siera started in coughing, as he often did when he finished one of his monologues. Siera, like many retired stone cutters, was a victim of silicosis from years of breathing in the marble, granite, and sandstone dust kicked up by the chisel.

Red took up the thread:

"That's what I understand. A lifelong professional student. Here on a family fortune."

"Something like that." Siera coughed. And coughed.

"Mr Butt is also, beyond any and all doubt, the King

of all Wisconsin Practical Jokers. He has pulled some of the wildest stunts I've ever heard of. And these things were elaborate. Thought out." Red said, and then he shook his head in unfeigned respect. Siera nodded, and added:

"Yes, I've known him to do those things. Sometimes they would end up in the papers."

"Right" said Red. "Case in point. I remember when he got on the phone--some people say he did the whole thing from that phone over there in the back of this building. He called every university big wig, making up names, making up voices, pretending to be somebody's secretary, calling to remind them about the special meeting to be held in Music Hall, over on Park Street at 7 PM tonight. The president of the university, the chancellor, the deans, the members of the Board of Regents, heads of the unions, members of the State Assembly and the Senate, all of them and more were called by Cy. Most of them came! And when they got there nobody knew what was happening. It was utter chaos! They all went nuts! Yelling at each other."

"Well, you called me to come!"

"No! Your secretary called ME, you imbecile!" said one dean to another.

Meanwhile, it was a lovely Spring evening, with a breeze blowing up Park Street, from the Memorial Union and Lake Mendota. A block away, at the jewel-box-like Music Hall, only building on campus admired by alumnus Frank Lloyd Wright, was a jumble of parked cars and men and women milling about, some speechifying, some standing stock still staring off into space, angry at being had. Meanwhile, high up in an oak tree, about a thousand feet away, in the yard of the

Education Building, was Cy Butt, laughing uproariously.

"I remember that." said Siera. Chuckling. Then coughing.

"I do too." said Red.

Cy Butt returned to the bar, sitting again upon the same stool, before the now empty whisky glass.

"Another wee dram for myself and get Mr. Siera one as well."

"Thank You Mr. Butt." said Siera.

"You're welcome Mr. Siera." responded Cy, in his most courtly manner.

The smoke-burnished, afternoon sunlight slanted in from west campus, from Cy's right. From the direction of Viroqua, and Vernon County, and all that Cy knew as a child, before he moved on to Madison, and his intellectual manhood (with still many side trips back to that natal, bucolic setting). South of University Avenue was the Greenbush, a jumble of rooming houses, small shops, vine-over-grown Italian sidewalks, labor temples, and Catholic churches.

Cy casually looked out the window. He watched the college crowd pass. He had long since given up any notion of joining them in any real professional sense. Although, he was a legal attorney at law in the State of Wisconsin, and did have occasional cases in the courts of Vernon and Dane Counties, most of these were concerning his drinking buddies, run afoul of the law. He was too old now to think of a great career, although he was happy the way things had turned out. He was able to perform an occasional public intellectual demonstration, and he still spent hours on end in the stacks of the university library, often times after sampling exotic liquors on State Street.

Anyway, despite his presence in at least one class each semester, he was content instead to poke at life with a sharp stick.

"Mr. Butt?" said the bartender, quite suddenly. "Can I tell you something?"

The bar tender, who was named Red, continued:

"There was a guy in here asking about you and he gave me the creeps."

Red was a tall, thin, almost gangly figure of a man, perhaps in his forties, who was largely bald, with a fringe of short brown hair streaked in gray. In better light than in this bar, his face could be seen as deeply tanned.

"Mr. Butt, this man was all dressed in gray. Wore a derby --also gray. He was a big man. He was hairless, except for a gray mustache and beard. Sort of a Van Dyke."

Cy listened very carefully. Looking at Red, nodding. Trying to coax more information out of him, a practice Cy had long ago learned in law school here on the U.W. campus. Part of this strategy was his very deliberate swirling of his drink around in his glass. The brown I.W. Harper whiskey and water (no ice, "That way they can't hear you coming!" Cy would cackle) swirled together like two dancers beginning to embrace, and Cy's blue eyes would try to direct the attention of his listeners to the effect. As a hypnosis tool. It was not working today. Red was intent on the story he had to tell.

"He was also asking about one of those old murders you are always poking around in. The one of that little Italian girl years ago in the Greenbush." continued Red.

"Bonnie DiMarco" said Cy.

Old man Siera's head rose from his contemplation of his drink and he quietly took in the conversation.

"Right." replied Red, wiping the bar with a rag and nodding for emphasis.

"What did he seem to know about that?"

"Well, he seemed to know that he didn't want you checking it out very much."

"I guess that means I'm on the right track." said Cy.

"What track would that be, Mr. Butt?"

"Well, it has occurred to me, while paging through the back issues of local newspapers over at the State Historical Society, that there have been a number of unsolved murders of women in the southern half of Wisconsin. And not just murders, but murders involving a considerable amount of lifting and carrying around of the victim to other, unknown locations. For God knows what purposes. Bonnie DiMarco is just one of them. Taken from her parents' home in the Greenbush in the middle of the night with nobody noticing, not even the family dog barking. Taken someplace for a day or two. Then she pops up floating in Lake Monona, a hundred feet from shore, a quarter of a mile from her home. Every house within ten blocks had been searched, every resident questioned. Nothing. Zilch. To this day they don't know who did it."

"Isn't that the one where that creepy old guy....uh..." probed Red.

"Coonskin Jackson? Yes, he confessed, and then he recanted, then he confessed again. They locked him up in Waupun State Prison on the basis of the confession, and then from the second the cell door shuts behind him he starts saying that he didn't do it and he was scared to say who did. He finally died in prison about ten years back."

"You don't think he did it then?"

"I think he was in on it, but I also think he had help. He had to have help getting her out of that house, help transporting her, and finally he had no location where to store the body for two days. His own house was a couple of blocks away, but he had a house full of kids himself, hard to hide a dead kid in a place like that. Plus his house was searched. There was some other location, and there must have been someone who helped him take her to that location."

"You know.." began Mr. Siera, rather softly: "..at the time some people said that the family was in on the murder. They even tried to prosecute the father, in the end without success. Thank God, for that. The man was my brother-in-law, and was innocent!" Siera concluded these remarks with a quick, but forceful fist bump to the bar. And then he coughed, while everybody listened quietly. Then he continued:

"Her funeral was held at St. James. Biggest funeral for a child ever held in Madison. She had six little girls dressed in white for her pallbeaers. Other little girls carried flowers." Siera began to weep softly. And then he quietly got up and left the bar, gently, silently waving goodbye to the other two men.

For quite a while nothing was said. Red broke the silence: "Mr. Butt, are there other such murders? That one was quite a while back."

"Okay, how about the murder of Louise Carlson in Lead Point in 1927?" Cy said as he swirled his whiskey around in his glass, gazing at it intently.

"Little before my time, Mr. Butt." said Red.

Cy suddenly switched his intent gaze from the whiskey to Red, who felt a brief shudder at the force of those narrowed eyes. "Okay, here's the particulars: pretty high school girl disappears from the school library in the middle of the day. The next day, her ritually tortured corpse was found nailed to a cross overlooking the Wisconsin River, thirty miles away."

"I've never heard about that one, ." said the incredulous Red.

"I'm not surprised." said Cy. " Authorities made a deliberate effort to bury the whole investigation. Local press accounts referred to it as a "farm accident". Nobody explained how the shy, bookish daughter of a hardware store owner should die in a farm accident when she's never milked a cow in her life, and nobody saw her anywhere near a farm on the day of her disappearance."

"How did you find out about it?" Asked Red.

"Maker's Mark." Answered Cy evenly.

"Excuse me." Said Red.

"I discovered that the nighttime dispatcher at the Sheriff's Office was a big fan of that rather hard to acquire Kentucky bourbon. So, he let me rifle the old case files, while he sipped. He also told me a few tidbits--such as the fact that considering the distance traveled, the inaccessibility of the location, the weight of the cross, etc., a minimum of three men would have been necessary to carry out the operation.

Mentioning bourbon whiskey made Cy wish he were sitting somewhere closer to the bathroom. He gazed out onto University Avenue at the passing knots of students, some of whom would turn their heads and crane their necks to see into the dimly lit bar. They could really make out nothing, but sometimes Cy liked to pretend they saw everything, deep into the depths of the narrow cave made by the bar on the west side of the building and the booths on the east side, hardly far enough apart for a couple to dance through. Not that this was much of an establishment for dancing, but it had been known to happen. Mostly in a cramped open area in the rear of the business next to the bathrooms, where two or three couples could safely dance, if not too inconvenienced by the pool table and the jukebox. This was a college town after all. And across University Avenue begins the Greenbush, the neighborhood of cheap rooming houses for students and inexpensive dwellings for families along the railroad tracks, a high percentage of which families were of Italian extraction, some of whom were descended from the sculptors and stone craftsmen the State of Wisconsin brought to Madison at the turn of the century to sumptuously rebuild the burned down state capitol building.

Suddenly, the outside door of the bar opened and somebody entered. Cy and Red gazed in astonishment into the glow of the afternoon Sun, out of which a dwarfish, hunched figure emerged. Cy immediately recognized his friend, U.F.O. book publisher Ken Starky, who operated a small press pulp magazine of the occult and mysterious, out of a print shop in Platteville, Wisconsin. He did have a sort of stringy black mustache, but no goatee.

Cy quickly turned back to Red, saying: "Was this the guy you say was asking about me?" And Red shook his head and seemed still doubtful about the approaching figure, who was now smiling and heading straight for Cy, who now said to Red, quietly, conspiratorially: "Too bad it wasn't." And then at the top of his voice: "HI! KEN!!!By God! Good to see ya!!!!How ya doin' fella!!!"

The two old friends then got into a bizarre backslapping and hand shaking ritual which Red found hilarious.

"What brings you to the big city? Red, get my friend Ken here a drink. I have birthday in two days. October sixteenth. What are you drinking, Ken?"

"Wine, red wine." said Ken with a shake of his head and a sort of smirk.

The noted publisher of UFO and paranormal magazines was brought to Madison by a quest it seems. An old man he knew in Platteville was on his death bed and spitting out legends about a secret tunnel somewhere in Madison.

Now Cy knew a lot about a lot of tunnels here, there, everywhere. He wanted Ken to be a bit more specific:

"A tunnel going from Lake Mendota to Lake Monona--supposedly dug during the Civil War"

"Ya," said Cy, swilling some more I.W. Harper meaningfully before he said: "I know just what you are talking about."

"Why was this built?"

"Nobody knows for sure. And it probably predates the Civil War, parts of it at least. And was originally used by runaway slaves. Parts of it. Parts of it have been built later."

"And a religion used it?" Ken asked dramatically. The wine was getting to him already. He probably wasn't used to it. Cy would have to make a note of that for later times. For the moment, Cy decided to direct his friend out the back door before the college boys began to drift in off University Avenue.

"Yes, and no." said Cy, as calmly, legalistically as he could. He was not trained as a lawyer for nothing.

"But they were a damned human sacrifice cult, right? Am I wrong Cy?"

"Exnay, Ken, old boy, exnay. I think we are all friends here but you shouldn't go around shouting stuff like that in the big city. You ain't back home on the farm now." said Cy.

"I know Cy. I'll quiet down. but I've just found out some pieces of this story just this week. And I'm here in town to check it out at a library or something. What have they got?"

"Well, save your time, Ken. I've been there before you and I assure you the big boys have covered up their tracks very well."

"No shit?" asked Ken.

"No shit." said Cy. "Nothing about inter-lake tunnels in local libraries. I've checked."

"Buy you a drink? " asked Ken.

"Let's go some place where you and I can drink for free." said Cy. And without a word, Cy rose from his bar stool and silently, stealthily began to walk towards the rear door of the establishment. Finally, he cocked his head back at Ken, put one index finger to his nose and motioned for him to follow. And Ken readily did. Cy gave a wave to Red as they exited. Red waved back in a slow, dignified salute of his hand from his forehead.

And Cy and Ken headed back to Cy's tiny Langdon Street apartment, a few blocks away, where Cy did a lot of drinking and talking, and Ken tried to interest him in his story of Enoch and mysterious space beings from Africa. Late in the night, Ken sacked out on a book covered couch and Cy headed for bed.

Chapter 10
Springfield Corners, north of Madison, Wis.
Thursday, Oct 15, 1953
2:15 A.M.

Bernard and Ned Lein were in a pasture of a sheep farm, nestled along Highway 12. They had just killed a ram. Bernard had shot the unsuspecting beast with his pistol and Ned was in the process of chopping off its head with an axe.

"Try to be a bit more careful this time, Ned." said Bernard, who stood aside, calmly smoking a cigarette, careful to not get any blood or manure on his pants or sports coat. Ned, in his ever present, greasy, smelly denim pants, jacket and shirt gave every impression of enjoying the splatter of the blood and flesh as he swung the axe viciously through flesh and bone.

"If you want to get your hands dirty come on in." said Ned, in a clear level tone, totally unlike, his normal gruff mumble.

"Just telling you that the Master isn't planning to eat this thing. It has to look good for the ceremony." whined Bernard, almost in a whisper, because he had noticed a light come on in the farm house far across the field, built into the tree decked slope of a hill. "Hurry it up though," added Bernard. At that very moment they saw the headlights of the police car.

"Get a move on Ned. Let's finish this up and get out of here. I'll take care of him."

Ned had parked his pickup truck off the road, next to Highway 12. Other cars had passed and nobody had noticed them out here in the field, a little below the road. But this police car was slowing up as if he were taking a look at the truck. Bernard began to walk swiftly across the pasture, his hand dipped casually down into his plaid sports coat. Ned made the last few chops on the ram's neck, dislodged the head from the body, and picked up the bloody mess, shoving it into a burlap sack he opened with his other hand.

The police car parked behind Ned's truck and the car door opened and closed. A middle-aged male in khaki pants, work shirt and overcoat advanced upon the truck. Bernard correctly sized him as a county cop, with police radio but no back up. Bernard figured that the gunshot had awakened the farmer nearby and he had called the cop. Another gunshot and a quick exit was what was called for.

An hour later, Ned's pickup truck entered the garage of a closed brewery building, a dark red brick mountain, next to Lake Monona, the smaller of the two isthmus lakes, on the near east side of Madison. Ned and Bernard were exiting the truck as the Master came trudging down the long, dark, stone stairway. His considerable bulk was not hidden by his gray suit. His immense round head was hairless except for a well trimmed Van Dyke beard. He smoked a hand rolled cigarette of some kind in a long ebony cigarette holder.

"We had to kill a cop." said Bernard.

"I heard that on the police radio." replied the Master. Blowing a cloud of smoke casually into the dimness of the garage "Well, no harm came of it. He did not radio in your license plate before... he stopped transmitting. Good work boys." He patted an appreciative Bernard on the shoulders. He fondly placed his arm around a shyly smiling Ned.

Ned nodded proudly as he looked at the canvas tarps in the box of the truck.

"Oh that's right." said the Master. " Is that where the ram's head is now?"

"Yes sir," said Ned. "Look in the burlap sack."

The Master opened the sack and hefted out the bloody ram's head.

"A splendid specimen, good work Neddie" said the Master, warmly, smiling at Ned, gently patting the stubble beard on the man's near cheek.

Ned shot an almost challenging look over at Bernard with a cocky, toothless grin. Bernard just stuck his hands in his sports coat pockets and nonchalantly sucked his teeth like Humphrey Bogart.

The Master ignored this jealousy among his underlings and broached a new project for them:

"I've got a pick up for you to make later today, here in Madison, for delivery up to the round barn in Vernon County. We are going to have a preliminary ceremony, preparatory to the offer of the virgin sacrifice later this month.   We are offering this ram's head and a supplicant for training. Moreover the anniversary of a very important date is coming up for me."

Suddenly, the Master's words were interrupted by a chattering sound and an explosion of gray fur coming down the curved stone stairway. The Master's marmoset skittered down the steps and across the garage to perch upon his owner's shoulder. The bald, fat man crooned to his pet, rubbing beneath his chin with his finger tips. Both Bernard and Ned looked on longingly.

"Get the Oldsmobile ready for a trip north. Clean up the ram's head and pack it in ice. We'll discuss this later" And with these words, the Master, with his marmoset on his shoulder and wreathes of smoke trailing behind, made the long climb up the circular stone staircase. At the top of the stairs was an enormous dark oak door, which he opened and closed behind him.

He was now in a large, high ceiling room. High stone walls were on three sides, but on the side nearest Lake Monona, the wall came up only waist height, making the room a sort of large balcony with a striking view of the floodlit, white, marble dome of the Wisconsin State Capitol towering above the city, the isthmus, and the lakes.

The stone floor of the room sloped sharply toward the lake, and the ceiling was much higher away from the lake than at the side facing the lake. The room gave the impression of shrinking away from the lake. The room had been used to facilitate the outside storage of barrels full of liquids. Small drainage holes penetrated the balcony wall.

Near the balcony wall stood a wrought iron coffee table and two wooden padded barrel chairs. In the occupied chair sat the assistant District Attorney of Vernon County Malcolm Prentiss. The Master sat down without a word to Prentiss and began to contently study the shimmering moon-lit surface of Lake Monona, all the while sending wafts of smoke in that direction, elegantly cradling his cigarette holder between two fingers. Finally, Prentiss broke the silence:

"Master, I think we are going to have to do something about Cy Butt." he said.

"That is my intention today." said the Master.

"We need to kill him, Master." said Prentiss with all the cold hardness he dared muster, hoping that the Master noticed this deliberate effort in the guise of submission.

In a bored, off hand fashion, the Master replied:

"It's ridiculous to kill him. He is of no consequence. Just an old drunk. No one really regards him with any respect or credibility . He does however have a good brain and we will offer that to our new allies."

"Hmmmmm...." said Prentiss.

"Our allies insist however that we do have to kill off that old nigger in Platteville. He is too much of a blabbermouth and people *do* listen to him." added the Master with a decisive blast of cigarette smoke aimed westward, in the general direction of Platteville.

"Master, is it wise to keep killing these people?" asked Prentiss.

The Master ignored the basic question and launched into a sermon:

"Today is an anniversary for me. Since October 15, 1915 I have been on a quest, mostly around here in Madison, but really worldwide, to make genuine contact with advanced life forms from other relativities. I met and was initiated into our cult here in Madison by the great Magus--Terrance Mulhaire." the Master intoned. "And on that occasion, and others, we made contact with these life forms.." he let it drop, breathlessly.

"Really, Sir? The great Mulhaire initiated you here in Madison? I thought it was in England or Paris with his other great adepts." asked Prentiss, eagerly playing the acolyte.

"Oh, I went there in time too. But I first met him here in Madison as he was traveling cross country visiting his temples in New York, Detroit, Chicago, Minneapolis, Seattle. We actually met at a restaurant in the train station. He noticed that I was reading a book by Aleister Crowley. I was taking courses at the university here."

Chapter 11
Madison, Wis.,
Thursday, October 15, 1953
10:00 A.M.

Student voices, car horns, and music could be heard from various directions as Cy and Ken walked down shrub overgrown Hawthorne Court, which was still damp from the morning fog off Lake Mendota. It was one of a number of quaint byways twisting through the rooming houses between State Street and University Avenue. There were walled gardens and brick and stone walk ways, all overarched by a number of spreading trees of good size and age. Legendary eccentrics dwelt back in these regions, and Cy knew them all well. There were translators of ancient Greek wedged next to bookbinders next to sculptors of colored concrete next to concert violinists. The smells of oil paints, Indian curry, and bizarre cigarette smoke danced to the polyphony of violins, bongos, and jazz records.

They entered a courtyard of a particularly exotic variety. Ken studied the plants growing in numerous garden patches. There were strange, bulbous things--multicolored--hanging from vines which were tied to the trunks of small trees. The trees had fragrant, unfamiliar leaves which Ken thought were particularly striking. And he reached out to touch one. But Cy, wordlessly, motioned him not to.

Cy led them up a stone stairway climbing from the courtyard, up the side of an old stone building, and around the building for a floor and a half to an obscure door, itself shielded by a concrete lattice. The door appeared to be of wood, but of a type so old, so shellacked, repainted, and preserved that it was almost stone-like. Attached to the door, although by no visible nails, was this sign:

"Professor R. .M. Alterweise: Translator; Herbalist; Ethnographer; Notary Public; Book Binder; Horoscopes Cast; Genealogist."

Cy lifted a metal door knocker in the center of the door and knocked three times. Three knocks answered on the other side of the door, almost immediately.

The door then opened.

The old Prof stood there, all 5 feet of him, in a dressing gown and topped by a red (yellow) tasseled fez.

"I knew you were coming before you ever made the first knock." said the Prof's rich Vienna voice.

"I knew you would. The bartender at Niño's called you last night, right?"

"That's it exactly, Cy. What do you think. I'm Nostradamus, up here, gazing into the future in a bowl of water?"

"Can you see the past then?"

"Only in a glass of beer."

"Good, don't mind if I do. Except make it whiskey

please."

"I. W. Harper, if I recall. No ice"

"That's it, Prof."

Cy and Ken sat down on a davenport in the tiny sitting room, which actually was a sort of alcove from a much larger room, which burrowed deep into the apartment in the form of an enormous library. The alcove was one of the few non book-lined areas of the apartment. Both men studied the artifacts surrounding them. One wall was dominated by a Navajo-looking blanket, which actually came from Africa, Cy had learned--from a place called Mopti near the Sahara. Another wall had a sort of tapestry. The figures therein depicted a Medieval hunting scene. Mounted nobles accompanied by thin greyhound-like dogs unsuccessfully pursing a clever fox, making his exit on one lower corner.

The Prof came back into the room from an adjacent kitchen, carrying a bottle of beer for himself , a glass of whiskey for Cy, and a glass of wine for Ken.

"I neglected my manners just now," said the Prof. "I took the liberty of asking the bartender what you were drinking so I didn't even bother to ask what you were drinking, sir." the Prof directed this remark to Ken. "Cy, you must introduce us."

"My pleasure, Prof, this is Ken Starky. Ken, the Prof. Prof, Ken runs a UFO magazine out of Platteville."

"It's more than a UFO magazine, Cy. " Ken insisted.

"Indeed it is, " said Cy.

"And yes, I would very much like to drink your wine." said Ken.

"I will give it to you then." said the Prof, bowing in a theatrical manner, and, after serving them their drinks, he took a seat in a leather covered, overstuffed chair next to the door. "Have a seat gentlemen. I think we have much to talk about."

Cy and Ken took chairs near the Prof and sat down, instinctively knowing they were going to listen for a while.

"You, Cy, have made a great enemy." The Prof flourished grandly with his hand to emphasize his words, and to indicate to Cy, that questions were permissible.

"Not another one." chuckled Cy.

"This is no laughing matter. This is a man who made use of his years of education. Except he actually got degrees."

"I became a lawyer." interjected Cy.

"That is true. For what it is worth." Prof stretched this out, said with a sigh: "But his studies were done not just at a Midwestern cow school--as your classmates say some times about this sainted University here between the Two Lakes. The man we are talking about is quite possibly the most evil villain in Wisconsin. He indeed is a very dangerous man. One of the most powerful and yet most unknown men in this state. He is man with all kinds of ancient occult wisdom. And he acquired them from all over the world-- America, Europe, Asia, specifically India, even Tibet. But he is also a self made millionaire from the arms industry, stock market, and other nefarious enterprises. Moreover, he is a licensed architect-- trained by the great man, Frank Lloyd Wright himself. As I was, once. Many years ago. He and I studied together on a number of occasions, over the years, in one or another field of learning. In fact, he has a range of learning almost equal to myself. And if I had bothered to go out in the world instead of staying here and reading about the world, I wonder sometimes if our careers might have run parallel. But that is hard to say. Impossible, really."

"Have you ever told the cops about this guy? You got any evidence on him?" asked Cy.

"I have told them, numerous times over the years. The reaction was always derisive laughter." said the Prof.

"Where does this guy live?" asked Cy.

"Here in Madison, I believe, and other places." said the Prof.

"How long has he lived here?" asked Cy.

"He was living here when I first arrived in 1920." answered the Prof.

"How is it that I have never met him." asked Cy, genuinely puzzled.

"He probably didn't want you to meet him." said the Prof with a chuckle. Then he continued:

" Plus he has been in and out of town a lot over the years, traveling various places. I've had reports on him from mutual acquaintances for years. But then, on the other hand, I'm sure you have met him many times over the years. Yet you just didn't focus on him. Because he didn't want you to. He is an expert at Eastern mind control techniques and he would certainly try to remain hidden from a wild man such as yourself. Until the time comes to make his appearance. I think he is very close to that indeed."

"How old is he?" asked Cy.

"Ageless, as far as I know. He has been very good at concealing his origins. Today in fact is a significant day for this man. An important man came through Madison on October 15, 1915." said the Prof.

"Who?" Cy cocked his head to one side, and studied the swirls inside his whiskey glass as he asked this of the Prof.

"Terrance Mulhaire." said the Prof suddenly. "He wrote his great poem "The Black Rose" here in Madison, on that very date. At least that is the date the official text opens with."

"Mulhaire," said Cy, "Who is he? Never heard of him."

"Well, literature and the fine arts is one area I've always said you neglected in your studies, Cy." said the Prof.

"Well, there is no there there." Cy cackled. "Nothing you can hang your hat on."

"Well, you might be right. And Mulhaire was even more esoteric than most. He engaged in automatic writing, spirit writing, other such things. He founded a cult which existed here for some years. I myself attended some of its sessions in the 1920s. I think they folded up during the great depression. They would meet at an old brewery building next to Lake Monona, over on the east side. He moved to the west coast where there is always a plentiful supply of potential members for such groups. He finally died in a mysterious explosion which may have been a suicide, maybe was the result of a mystical thing gone wrong." the Prof reminisced.

"What kinds of things did they do? Spiritualism?" snickered Cy.

"Some believe that they did workings like those of Aleister Crowley." replied the Prof.

"What do you mean?" asked Cy, now intrigued.

"They may have called up beings from other worlds." said the Prof.

"My God Prof! This is incredible!" said Cy. "Are you talking about gods? Or perhaps demons?" he continued.

"I'm not sure. Maybe that is what gods are." pondered the Prof.

"Fascinating Prof. But this isn't why we've come here to see you." said Cy.

"It isn't? Then why are you here?" asked the Prof incredulously.

"Kenny here had a question about a network of tunnels he's heard about here in Madison." said Cy.

"Oh, that old thing. Yes. Well, that's involved, it all is, here in Madison. This little town with a great big soul, but not a very big heart! Hehe! I must remember that one! Yes, the tunnel is involved with this man as well. The whole bunch of them used it as an escape route any number of times. That's how they got Bonnie DiMarco away and out into the lake where they killed her. These very same people, Cy. So, beware. That murder of a virgin out in a lake is something out of Sir James Frazier and *The Golden Bough*. I've got it in the next room. It's a scapegoat ritual. Usually performed to cleanse the land of evil. I think there's been rather a lot of that sort of thing going on in Wisconsin over the years. Mysterious murders that come out of nowhere. Often of young girls."

"Such as Bonnie DiMarco. I've been looking into that. Just for the hell of it--" said Cy.

"And just for the hell of it, you've kicked over a big hornets' nest and you don't even know it, do you? Oh well, the hero has to go out questing for the monster does he not?" The Prof laughed contemptuously.

"Well, Red told me something about some guy coming around asking questions at the bar." interjected Cy.

"Well, that is the very man I've been referring to. That happened days ago. Where have you been anyway? I've actually tried to reach you."

"I was back in Viroqua for a while."

"Well, that might make a good hideout from these people, but not for long. " said the Prof.

"Who the hell are you talking about?" asked Cy, a measure put off.

"An evil cabal of men, and some women, who have operated a secret cult here in the heart of Madison for decades!" said the Prof, rocking back in his chair, hugging himself as if to acquire the warmth, but really did it as a sort of habit.

"People in league with this evil genius? Who are these people? A bunch of weirdoes, fringe characters?" Cy asked--amazed that he had never suspected such a secret right here in Wisconsin's center of legal and intellectual power.

"Some of them are. They consist of powerful industrialists, politicians, bureaucrats, university officials, businessmen." said the Prof., no longer rocking himself, but just looking quietly at Cy.

"And what do they do?" asked Cy.

"They murder, they steal, they forge and blackmail, all to attain any end their evil cult needs to acquire wealth and power." said the Prof. now looking at the floor.

"Are you serious about this?" asked Cy.

"Deadly serious. And these are the people you have sniffing around you. The man in the gray derby is just one of them, but he is the chief one. And my recommendation is to do all you can to avoid them." said the Prof, now nodding his head fervently and looking Cy in the eyes.

"Hmmm," said Cy. "This bunch sounds to me like they need their ears pinned back a bit."

"I thought you might say something like that. That's why I was reluctant to say anything to you about it."

"Well, I'm glad you did. This might be my next big project."

"I'm glad I did too. That way when they fish your headless body out of Lake Mendota, I'll feel a little less guilty when I cut and paste into my scrapbook the tiny news item the *Capital Times* will print about you."

"No need for you to feel any guilt."

"No, no need at all. And I won't, don't worry. The hero must go out in quest of the monster," said the Prof as he flashed a grim smile to Cy.

"Who says that?" asked Cy.

"A scholar named Campbell." and then the Prof got up from his chair as if to search for something in one of the book shelves along the floor.

Ken Starky, who had hitherto been silent during the Prof's extraordinary pronouncements, took this opportunity to timidly direct the conversation to the topic he had come here seeking information on:

"So, then, there is a tunnel between the two lakes?"

"There are tunnels and caves all over Wisconsin, all over the Driftless area. The entire region is a vast *Alka-Seltzer* tablet, sunk into the sedimentary detritus of eons of warm, tropical seas, lolling across what is now the Midwest. Made of various forms of limestone, all of it dissolving very slowly, gradually, over hundreds of millions of years, and fissures or chambers open up here and there beneath stronger surface layers. Corridors and passages can be found, and traversed...." The Prof's voice drifted off pleasantly as he continued to shuffle along the book shelf. He was deep in thought, as if trying to remember something.

"What are you looking for Prof? I know you're not looking for a drink for me." Cy rose, deliberately, glass in hand and headed for the library room, where he knew the whiskey to be.

"Ahhhhh. Here, yes. Right here," The Prof said. "*The Golden Bough.*" He seated himself near the light with his battered spectacles perched precariously on his bony nose: "Yes, yes, right here. This footnote says it very nicely:

'A scapegoat, on the other hand, is an animal or human being used in public ceremonies to remove the taint or impairment consequent upon which, for one reason or other cannot be saddled upon a particular individual. Such a scapegoat is a means of 'cleansing' a community of a collective stain which cannot be wiped out by the normal procedure of individual penitence, restitution, and reform."

The Prof interjected: "And these words are in Italics:

'"The *execution* or *despatch*--

The Prof interjected:

"Note how he spells dispatch, the language changes before our very eyes."

"'--of it is always and necessarily accompanied by a blanket public confession.'"

The Prof laid the book at his knee and looked at Cy and

Ken, as if they were a pair of snotty nosed school boys in a country school:

"So, what do we see in that? Hmmm. Hmmmph! Cy, your ideas!"

"They are killing people to make themselves feel better?"

"Simple minded. But true! Yet, it is far more complex. Ken, you have been neglected far too long."

Ken noticeably squirmed in his chair.

"Now, Ken, for some reason, you have brought us all together."

"No, I haven't. I just stopped off at that bar yesterday looking for Cy. I know he often hangs out there. I didn't plan to spend the night--"

"No." continued the Prof, now very reassuringly. "You didn't know you were the cause. But you were the cause. We wouldn't be speaking of these matters if you had not sought out Cy. What was it made you seek him out?"

Ken, relaxed. At last sure that HIS problem would now receive some attention:

"I know an old guy in Platteville. Just a bag of bones, skinny, over ninety years old. He might have been a freed slave, or at least the child of one. He was a carpenter once. Built barns, round barns. And he's been living in a little apartment behind my book shop. I let him live there for free in exchange for him watching over the place. Cleaning up. Puttering. Weeds, maybe shovel sidewalks. Sometimes he did a little carpentry. He is ninety, but he does like to work. Has all his life. And besides, I pay all the utilities. Now he is staying in my own apartment the loft over the store."

"I'm sure you are good to this man." responded the

Professor. "But what did he say to you that is so important that you come here to tell us about it in Madison?"

"Well, he said creatures from another planet live in a tunnel under Madison!"

Suddenly, to the shock of all, the telephone rang.

The rotund Prof found it necessary to arise and waddle over to the phone and answer it. He could hear the Prof engaged in sincere, business-like, formal conversation. He also heard his own name mentioned. Finally, the Prof turned and looked toward him and said:

"Cy, it's for you."

When Cy got on the line he found himself talking with a young, whiny voice:

"Mr. Butt. I'm a friend of Tommy Torgerson, you got him off that muffler charge in Viroqua. Well I've got the same kind of charge on me in Richland County. And I know the only reason they ticketed me is because they know I'm going to college in Madison and haven't got the time to fight the charge."

Damned thought Cy. Damned speed traps.

"Can I just talk to you a second. My car is parked next to the 602 Club on University and I have to go to work soon. It won't take much time."

Cy made his quick apologies to Ken and the Prof, assuring them he would be gone for just a few minutes.

"I'll be right around the corner, at the 602 Club."

Cy turned off Hawthorne Court onto Francis Street. So focused was he upon University Avenue ahead that he did not at all notice a small figure in a plaid sports coat emerge from an obscure doorway. Before Cy recognized Bernard from the Vernon County courtroom the weasel-faced man pulled a small gun out of his coat pocket and shoved it into Cy's side.

"Now shut up and get going" And he shoved Cy Butt roughly into the direction of a black Oldsmobile car parked along Francis Street. The back door of the car opened, and a wall of a man waited inside, also with a gun in his hands.

"Get in Mr. Butt." said an immense gray suited man with a gray beard and mustache but no other hair on his carefully shaved head. This man held a somewhat larger gun than the one Cy felt being shoved into his back. And Cy had no choice but to obey these two guns. He swiftly found himself stuffed into the back seat of the car, which in another moment started up Francis Street and turned right onto University Avenue. Cy noticed the denim clad, toothless farmer from the courtroom behind the wheel. Ned looked into the rear view mirror and gazed upon Cy Butt. Ned grinned his toothless grin and quietly laughed. The young gangster looking guy sat to his right and the gray presence sat to his left.

Then with a bite of power, the car shoved everyone back in their seats as they pulled out onto University Avenue and headed north east. That was the precise moment that Cy felt a tiny prick on the left side his neck, which he had time to think was a mosquito, before he realized who was sitting there, and then all went dark.

As Cy regained consciousness, the first sensation he was aware of was the smell of cow manure. And not a faint, distant smell. This was a dramatic, fingers in the eye kind of smell.

And there was the vision of something hovering over him. A huge red mouth, but also black, brown, and now yellow.

Then he felt something on his face which was warm, oozing and above all wet--

"Right on his damned face! I'll be dogged! And he still lays there." said one male voice.

"Wait till she takes a piss!" said another male voice.

Cy knew somehow these voices were referring to him. Although at this point he still didn't have enough information to take much of a stand on anything--least of all his legs. He was becoming well aware of that. He now knew he was recumbent, on a hard surface, probably concrete. Probably in a cow barn. Perhaps fairly close to a cow, and it was a source of considerable amusement to at least two men. He had realized that when the liquid hit. He initially thought someone had thrown a drink in his face. But it was far more acrid and voluminous than that--

"There she goes!" both of the men laughed uproariously. Clearly this was part of the scheduled entertainment for them. Now if Cy could only find out in which theater he was playing. He rolled away from the torrent of liquid and found himself at the feet of a short, skinny, middle aged man with a gaunt, unshaven face. He was dressed in green work shirt and blue jeans and wore a crumpled baseball hat. This man opened his mouth in what Cy at first thought was going to be a smile and instead he made way for a squirt of tobacco juice which would have landed directly between Cy's eyes if he had not again rolled suddenly to one side. As it was, it only glanced his temple.

But this second roll turned him more in the

direction of the liquids and the oozings he had been receiving from the back end of the cow under which he had been when he woke up. And, suddenly--again with that warm, wet, oozing sensation on his face, which he now realized to be cow dung in its primordial state. He cast a quick glance at cow hind ends, which seemed to surround him in a circle. The cows were also strange looking, to Cy, used to the black and white Holsteins of Vernon County. They were in fact a uniform red color. And while farming was a bit out of Cy's line, he was observant enough to realize he had never seen cows that looked like that.

He was apparently being made sport of by some farm boys in a cow barn. The barn itself was rather odd, either Cy's field of vision had somehow wrapped itself into a circle, or else the barn itself was round.

Cy had got drunk in many strange places over the years. Once in a while he had done so in barns, mainly when trying to talk farm boys from the Kickapoo Valley into joining the baseball teams he used to manage. A guy gets himself into all kinds of fixes and bets and challenges in bars in places like Melvina and Kieler and Kellnersville--if you don't watch who you drink with (and Cy didn't). But try as he might he could not come up with any fragment of a recent drinking episode in a round barn.

There was instead something about a car ride--

"Oh don't try to recall all of us, Mr. Butt. I can see that look in your eyes." these words came from another face, a more distant one.

This was an older face, a more cultivated one, well shaven, in fact totally shaven except for a mustache and tiny Van Dyke, positioned just perfectly beneath the chin of a largely round visage. But this was not at all a friendly face. The eyes were openings into caverns the depths of which Cy knew he never wanted to see. And indeed, perhaps to keep Cy from seeing too far into his hideous eyes, the man moved his face about frequently, almost as if in a muscle tick True to the description he had received in the bar from Red, the man was dressed entirely in gray. Gray suit, gray derby, gray hair and mustache and beard. Definitely a sort of a Van Dyke. The overall effect was one of ashes, a creature of ashes, moving about on legs. On top of all this, he carried about on his shoulders a leashed primate of some kind. Cy later learned that this was a marmoset.

Meanwhile, hovering at this man's side was the weasely gunsel Cy now remembered from the car ride.

"Mister Butt..." intoned the man in gray. "While we have met, the pleasure was all mine. Each and every time, I assure you. In short I've seen you a number of times but you've never seen me. By choice. My choice. The cow barn --of course a deliberate part of the scene I've set up for you. For I present you with a tableau of life. Before us, the goddess of fertility, praised in every culture, renowned from civilization to civilization--the cow, the symbol of fertility and fecundity and nourishment. You have lived a life apart from that of your fellows. We have observed that. Oh, of course, you've had your college jollies. But you are alone, essentially alone. Have always been and will always be. Perhaps, and that is the decision you must make here, now."

Cy began to scoot himself away from the cow, slowly, using his elbows for traction. When he was what he considered to be a safe enough distance away from the bovine, he propped himself up on one elbow, and stared at the bearded man with as close to a jaunty expression he could muster and said:

"I can take a crappy joke as well as the next fellow, but I really object to your not introducing yourself to me." And then Cy turned away from the man as if he were not worth his trouble. The response was a swift kick in one of Cy's ribs, delivered by the weasley gunsel.

"Come now, Bernard. We must be a bit more cordial to our guest. He isn't a member of the state legislature after all." And the bearded man laughed uproariously at a private joke which apparently only he understood. The young gangster, stared fixedly at Cy.

The halfwit old farm hand also seemed transfixed by the scene. Drool formed at the corners of his largely toothless mouth as he almost seemed ready to say something to Butt. He even started to point, but was interrupted, as if in thought, by the commands of the man in gray:

"Ned, don't stare at him like that. It's impolite."

Bernard. Ned. Cy would have to remember the names and run them past Detective Monroe, if, and when he ever made it back to Madison alive. Cy was used to coming out of stupors in various conditions and he wasn't sure what he had been injected with, but he knew it was powerful. There was an odd ringing in his ears and his throat was quite dry.

"What kind of decision are you talking about, Mr.--- uh, what is it I call you?" queried Cy.

"Doctor will do, for now." the bearded man said. "Master, that is also applicable." The accent was at times Germanic and at other times strangely Southern.

Butt had met people in eastern Ohio with such speech inflections--eastern Ohio, where the Butt family coalesced before making the big move west to Wisconsin in the 1850s. Cy had been back to Zanesville, and Greenville, and other places where the Butts had migrated from--that is after they came from the State of Maryland, just after the Revolution, and before that they came from Ireland, in the mid 1770's. He had heard such strange mixtures of Germanic and Dixie--for that part of Ohio was not all that far from the influences of the South.

"You don't seem to flinch at my calling myself Master?" said the gray suited bearded guy. Cy realized that the man wanted a response.

"You call yourself Master, you say," said Cy, more preoccupied than anything. He had been in worse situations than this. Of that he was sure. Cy Butt had once been kidnapped by a bunch of Al Capone's gangsters, and taken up north and held prisoner in a cabin north of Hayword. Those were men who walked around with submachines under their arms all the time. From what Cy could tell he was being held prisoner by a gang of cow milkers led by a well dressed old fruit (backed up by a weasley gunsel.).

"Yes," the Master said, walking up to a nearby cow, putting his arm around her ample neck and making some sort of clucking sounds with his teeth to her clearly appreciative expression. This was definitely not the first time that man and that cow had met, thought Cy. "Yes, on October 15, 1915, in the train station of the City of Madison I met the man who would change my life. A man who was himself already a Magus, and who tutored me as a subordinate, if no less worthy station of Master, in our Order."

Order? thought Cy. That's what this is about? This guy is some kind of religious nut?

"Uh,..." said Cy, sort of playing for time until his brain completely cleared (he wasn't sure if it would, for a while). Cows, barn, guns. Some kind of gangland hangout like they used to have up north or over in the Kickapoo Valley during Prohibition. He's evidently run afoul of some gangster, without meaning to. Cy tried to stay on the good side of what people did not yet at this time in history call 'the Mafia', but which those on the inside clearly knew existed. And Cy knew it existed. The word Cy would have used at this time was "syndicate".

The cow barn set up was not something unknown to the nascent organized crime establishment of Wisconsin, at this time and before. A cow barn is a perfect place to hide all kinds of things. The place is wet, covered with and smelling like cow dung, plus full of numerous surly, gas, urine, and dung emitting bovines who are in the process of eating and don't much appreciate strangers. Only the most iron willed cops would conduct much of an investigation or search in such a place. Hence, such places in Wisconsin had become ideal hideouts for illegal liquor, cars, and people from Illinois and the Twin Cities since the advent of the Gangster Era in the 1930s.

But that was not what was involved here.

Cy began to feel that he should say something. So, he once again raised himself on one bony elbow, and while resting the opposite hand upon the weary, dung-streaked, and somewhat moth-eaten, brown, suit coat, Cy said with as much cockiness as he could muster: "Order Up!!"

"Dammit Master! I told you this was a big fat mistake!" said Bernard, who gave every indication of wanting to plant another shoe heel in Cy's ribs.

"That's Ok. Ok. Bernard. We are dealing with a hard case here. He has not had the spiritual advantages that you and I have had." said the bearded man.

"You can sure say that again." said Bernard, with a strange sincerity.

"Mr. Butt. Let me come right out with it."

"That's how I like it best. If I can get it at all."

The bearded man seemed to contemplate Cy's throw-away remark as if it had some sort of hidden meaning. Finally, he said:

"There is a world within your world, Mr. Butt. You have relentlessly and persistently refused to face it, although it has come face to face with you any number of times. You can be of use to us Mr. Butt. Your skills as a researcher, a quirky, somewhat disreputable lawyer with no particular political bent, as a man about town with no particular family responsibilities. And a man whose personal trust fund has been depleted somewhat by the ravages of post war inflation."

The man in gray was definitely right there. Although, it was a topic Cy rarely cared or bothered to think about, his lifetime project of self education on the inheritance of his late namesake grandfather was running into difficulty. The money just did not go as far as it used to. Particularly when you spent as freely as Cy did. The man in gray proceeded to quote to Cy his latest bank balances, down to today's interest accumulated. He also quoted his expenditures on rent, tuition, books, frivolity, and yes, food. It was all true, Cy was certain. And the trend was decidedly negative.

Cy could use some more money these days, on a fulltime basis. But what did this bunch of characters want for it?

"Do you want to hire me as a researcher?"

"I want to hire your soul."

"My what!? I got rid of that years ago!" Cy snickered this with a brave face of contempt, but there was some measure of discomfort inflexed in his voice, he knew it.

"Well, maybe you did. But I just want to hire that part of your brain where it used to be. There must have been dreams in your heart at one time. You must have been able to believe in something beyond this world once, something beyond the bottom of the bottle."

"Listen, if this is some kind of temperance lecture, believe you me I've heard them from experts. Real Bible pounders. Soul magnets. Men, and women, who could get people to run up to the stage screaming. You don't appear to have that kind of magnetism."

"I don't need to have that kind of magnetism. I can introduce you to someone far more powerful. Someone from another world. Someone I first began to serve when a man arrived in Madison, Wisconsin on October 15, 1915." As he said that, the Master turned away and walked to the center of the round barn. "Ned, will you help me ascend."

And Ned, the toothless farmer, joined the Master in the center of the barn and began pulling upon a pulley device Cy now noticed for the first time. Out of the hay strewn upon the round center of the barn a round platform rose up and up. It climbed above the heads of Cy and Bernard and the cows and took the two men up to the level of the hay mow. The Master then walked from the round platform across a narrow cat walk to the circular hay mow. Ned then pullied himself back to the barn floor.

From above the Master's voice thundered: "Now bring our supplicant.."

Supplicant, thought Cy. Well that must be me. And in another moment Ned and Bernard picked him up and carried him over to the round platform. While Bernard kept his gun jammed in Cy's ribs, Ned pulled the platform up into the air to the level of the round hay mow. When they reached the level of the cat walk Cy was stunned to find the hay mow totally devoid of hay. Instead he found himself face to face with the Master, now sitting on a sort of throne. His gray suit was now covered by a long black robe. His gray derby was replaced by a black cowl. The marmoset was no longer seen.

Two other men on somewhat smaller thrones were located two of the points of a five pointed star which (while incomplete due to the empty circle in the center) was suggested by chalk lines drawn on the wooden floor.

Cy's attention was drawn to another feature on the floor in front of the throne of the Master. This was the head of a ram. Blood oozed from underneath the evidently recently slain beast.

"Bring our supplicant to face the head of the ram." said the Master.

Cy felt himself being pushing across the cat walk by Bernard and Ned. The three came to a halt directly in front of the ram's head which was in front of the throne of the Master.

"Begin the clockwise circumambulation." said the Master, and Cy found himself propelled away from the

Master, to the right to the direction of another man, on a smaller throne, also wearing a robe and cowl. This man looked at Cy Butt and said:

"I invoke thee, the terrible and invisible gods who dwell in the void place of the Earth: Aiwas, Legba, Lebe, and Phalarthao. Hear me and make all spirits of earth and air serve me and be subject unto me, so that every Spirit of the firmament and of the ether may come forth, upon the Earth and under the Earth, on dry land, air, and in the water".

He then stood and pounded three times loudly on the floor of the hay mow with a staff he held. It took a while, but Cy came to recognize this man as none other than Assistant District Attorney Malcolm Prentiss.

"Continue the circumambulation." said the Master, and Cy and his two escorts continued to the right along the points of the five pointed star. At the next point another man sat on a small throne and he said:

"I invoke the terrible gods who dwell in the void place of the Sky: Roubriao, Mariodam, Balbnabaoth, Assalonai, Aphnaio, and Thoteth. Hear me spirits of air and water, be subject unto me, so that every Spirit of the firmament and of the ether may come forth, upon the Earth and under the Earth, on dry land, the air, and in the water."

He then stood and pounded loudly three times on the floor of the haymow with a staff he held. However, this man, from the tiny wisps of blond hair Cy perceived beneath the cowl and the fine Nordic features bore a remarkable resemblance to the lawyer from La Crosse Cy had seen defend Bernard in Vernon County Court.

"Finish the circumambulation." said the Master. Bernard and Ned pulled Cy again to the right, passing two points of the five pointed star and they all finished up standing in front of the ram's head which sat on the steps of the Master's throne.

"I call upon our teachers from the beyond to join us." said the Master.

What happened next was something for which Cy was never able to compose a realistic explanation. Seemingly out of the very texture and grain of the wooden plank walls of the hay mow, at the point that would have been the star point to the left of the Master, a figure materialized. This figure resembled nothing so much as an enormous Reptile on two legs, taller than a human, dark green shiny skin covered his body. He wore a black, silk robe. He was followed by a cluster of small, 3 and a half to 4 feet tall gray figures with heads larger in proportion to the rest of their bodies than adult humans. These figures stood in a circle to the left of the throne of the Master.

Cy tended to make his mind up quick and keep it that way. To the day he died, he basically rationalized that the scene he witnessed in that round hay mow was the result of some kind of complex theatrical effects complicated with the application of various drugs. The notion that he actually saw creatures from another world or existence was given no hospitality in Cy's mind whatsoever, and in fact was tossed into the gutter like an unruly, smelly, pauper from an elegant supper club.

Therefore, Cy was not only not afraid of what he was seeing but was growingly contemptuous of it. He also had to urinate, his normal condition.

Cy unzipped his pants and proceeded to urinate on the ram's head. "Happy birthday to me!" he said.

Bernard and Ned seemed to react the most

vigorously of anyone in the haymow.

"Crap." said Bernard.

"Keyriste" said Ned.

The Master simply wrinkled up his face and said to the giant reptile:

"Should I have him killed?"

"No", said the Reptilian. "Turn him lose somewhere and let him tell his story. Let him disrupt your enemies by just talking." These words were followed by a satisfied chuckle, and then a hiss.

And in a moment, the Master walked forward and Cy again felt a needle sting on his neck.

The Reptilian said to the Master (as Cy entered a haze): "You must acquire the receptive supplicant I ordered you to, no matter how much trouble it is."

Chapter 12
Saturday, October 17, 1953
Madison, Wis.

C y had few memories after that remark. And immediately after that, the circular top of the barn began to whirl about in a sort of cyclonic vortex. It was like looking down into the inside of a tornado, except he knew he was looking up at the ceiling of the circular barn. It was as if a vast tunnel were stretching up into the universe and he was flying upwards into it. And at his side, as if guiding him, was the Master. That was the last thing he remembered.

Then he woke up, sprawled across the lap of the statue of Abraham Lincoln in front of Bascom Hall, at the top of Bascom Hill. And he saw, through his bleary eyes, the upside-down visage of campus police officer Patrick O'Grady. Cy was amazed to find Officer O'Grady out here in outer space with him, and Abraham Lincoln. And he wasn't sure he should think such a thing. Then Cy realized that he himself was the one whose head was upside down and O'Grady was on the surface of the Earth. When O'Grady saw he was awake, he greeted Cy warmly with:

"Well now, Mr. Butt. So glad you could join us." and then O'Grady began to bang his night stick forcefully on the soles of Cy's shoes. He groaned: "I missed my birthday."

As Philio DeGarmo's car throatily puttered away from the Madison city police station near the Capitol Square, Cy Butt morosely watched the City of Madison disappear, and the cornfields of Dane County emerge. The young man drove his own slightly rusted Nash, rather than a State owned car, to the farming hamlet of Jena, southeast of the city. They parked in the nearly empty lot of a small tavern called "Lena's at Jena". Only a late model Cadillac waited in the lot.

The two men exited the car and Philio led the way to the front door of the establishment. As they entered, the intern waved away the plump, gray-haired woman who sat behind the bar, at the far end of the building. She never stirred from the arm chair she filled. She waved back, the flab of her arm danced as she waved. This had happened before. She turned up the volume to the radio broadcasting "Ma Perkins". The two men sat together at a booth near the front door .

They joined the diminutive, if dignified, Grover W. Townsend, Wisconsin's Attorney General, who sat alone at a booth, already awaiting for them:

"Well, Cy, been up to your escapades again I see," said the state's chief lawyer, with a chuckle, pointing meaningfully at the stains of cow manure still clinging to Cy's clothing.

"You owe me a new suit, Grover." said Cy tersely.

"You have not owned a new suit since one you purchased at Felix's Clothing Store in Viroqua, in December, 1938. A wedding of your nephew I believe." said Grover, matter of factly.

"By God Grover, I think you're right. And it's been a good piece of material."

"Don't worry Cy. The State will make it right." nodded Grover, magnanimously smiling.

"Well, farming is a new one on me, Grover." said Cy. "It's actually far worse than it looks."

"Actually, you might be surprised to learn that I know quite well how bad it is. Or at least I suspect I do. I suspect I know who it is you have been dealing with." said Grover with a mixture of dignity and zealotry.

"Who is this bastard, Grover? Have you ever heard of him?"

"I've heard vague rumors of such a powerful, evil man operating behind the scenes here in Wisconsin for years. But those who knew did not say, and those who said, did not know." Grover sighed.

"If they've committed crimes, and evidently they did, why doesn't it ever show up on police reports or get mentioned in court rooms." asked Cy.

"Oh, it gets mentioned, but you don't know what you are hearing. That's what I've finally concluded." mused Grover Townsend. "And sometimes it is just covered up, like that hearing in Viroqua."

"Did it originate here in Wisconsin?"

"No, I don't think so. Maybe not even in the United States, or even Europe. It's just been an evil thing floating about the world like a contagion. Taking root here, getting extirpated there."

"This guy seems to have some kind of religion behind him. I remember that much. I don't remember a lot. I got hit with far more than booze, Grover. It made me sleep through my birthday."

"We know exactly what you were hit with. Drugs used only by the Nazis and Chinese tong warriors, as far as my contacts in the FBI tell me."

"They know about this guy too?"

"I can't get a straight answer on that from them."

"Not even your big buddy J. Edgar? He won't give you the scoop?"

Grover, who shot Cy a cautionary glance, declined to respond except for a sort of cough. Cy could tell that Grover did not much appreciate his making light of his treasured contacts with the Bureau. Grover added, to shift the topic:

"We have checked out those two men you said were at that ceremony. Neither Assistant District Attorney Prentiss nor the lawyer in La Crosse have been in their respective offices for some days. Both are out of town, we are told. That is interesting." he said, looking at Cy meaningfully. Then, with relief, he directed his attention outside the taven to a squad car of the Madison Police Department which came to a slow stop in the gravel parking. All three men at the booth watched the famed Madison homicide detective Monroe P. Hammersley exit from the front passenger side. A uniformed officer sat behind the wheel and remained in the car. Hammersley was a slight figure, dressed in a black suit and tie. He was shorter than Townsend, who in turn was shorter than Cy. They were all three of them skinny, bony men. Hammersley walked with a pronounced limp. He step-hobbled his way across the expanse of the yellow graveled, rutted, and mud streaked parking lot. Hammersley seemed to be showing his age these days. He had, after all, been shot at least three times on duty, and one other time nobody ever said much about, but which might have had to do with one of his four marriages. He was certainly one of the last men in the entire State of Wisconsin to regularly wear a straw hat which he sported today. With his small, round glasses and the straw hat, he bore an uncanny resemblance to the 1920's silent film star Harold Lloyd. Except for the fact that his face was a sagging, sadder, wiser version of the youthful form.

A little bell over the door of the tavern ting-a-linged as Hammersley entered. He glanced up at it in a quick, nasty shot of his beady eyes. He waved the bar lady away as she looked up from her radio soap opera at the far end of the building. He walked slowly over to the booth occupied by Cy Butt and party. Wordlessly, he sat down in the booth and picked up the greasy menu of the establishment.

"What do you gents recommend?" he asked in his gravelly, nicotine-coated voice. Cy noted the ever present Old Gold cigarette in Hammersley's right hand--a hand heavily stained tobacco-brown.

As Grover Townsend contemplated Hammersley, it occurred to him that the detective was one of the few men he could think of who actually made Cy Butt look healthy. And right on cue, the Old Gold-inspired cough started up.

Without bothering to answer Hammersley's question, Grover asked:

"Any new word on the murder of the deputy?"

"Just the basics." Hammersley began, looking

inquisitively to Grover while nodding at Cy. Grover quietly nodded his approval for Hammersley to bring these matters up in front of Cy Butt. "Fifty year old county deputy, Norton Terwilliger, gets called in by a farmer on a trespassing complaint north of Springfield Corners. Some kind of vehicle was parked along the highway. A pickup truck we think. Down in the field two men, according to the foot prints, were decapitating a ram sheep down in a pasture--"

"What!?" asked Cy incredulously.

"My thought exactly Cy" said Grover, attempting to sooth Hammersley over his obvious irritation of being interrupted.

"That's right." continued Hammersley. "We found the body, sans head, down in the pasture. Then one of them shot the Deputy Terwilliger and they drove off."

"And now we have a kidnapping of a state investigator." said Grover looking at Monroe.

"Kidnapping my ass." guffawed Monroe.

"Well what would you call it?" asked Grover.

The two men let the matter drop. Monroe looked up from his menu, as if he were truly consulting it, and asked in a mock off hand manner:

"Well, Mr. Butt, we made a visit, didn't we, to the abortion parlor of old Doc Alterweise on Hawthorne Court--who is incidentally a known opium smoker--" said Monroe looking at Cy.

"He is an adjunct faculty member of the University. " said Cy, with a note of outrage.

"So is half the population of Madison." said Monroe.

"Besides. We didn't smoke any opium." Cy said. "Barely got around to any liquor before I was hauled away."

"Hauled away by a giant snake man?" asked Monroe derisively.

"Hey, Monroe. You don't think it is any more ridiculous than I do. I just lived through it." said Cy.

"So you are saying you believe this wizard or whatever he is..." Monroe began.

"The Master." Cy offered.

"Right, this Master conjured up a lizard and some little gray men out of the walls." asked Monroe.

"It was probably done with mirrors or something." said Cy. "Point is, they did it and maybe some of them really believe it's true. I for one don't. But they had a dead sheep head, and you got a dead sheep and you got a dead cop maybe these guys were around when the cop got killed too." said Cy, decisively.

"Monroe, I take it you don't believe in magic?" said Grover, with a wry look on his face as he delicately tapped together the tips of his fingers.

"Damned right I don't" said Hammersley, who dramatically inhaled a mouthful of tobacco smoke which he nearly spat out in the direction of ceiling, as if he were expelling a diseased thought or emotion.

"Nor do I Monroe, but I know what I saw." said Cy.

"I think Doc Alterweise knows more about this than he is telling." said Monroe decisively.

"You stay away from him Monroe, let Cy handle him." said Grover, smoothly, but firmly.

A short silence ensued, broken only by a sudden, unexpected question directed by Grover to the hitherto silent Philio:

"Tell me lad...what do you think?"

"Well, Sir. There have been examples of legitimate miracles recognized by the Vatican."

Monroe made a contemptuous snort. Cy and Grover ignored Monroe and both looked at Philio, both deliberately conveying great interest with their facial expressions. The tall, thin, boy in a blond crew cut towered over his companions at the table, but he knew he was decidedly playing out of his league. Six weeks ago he was studying for his bar exam.

"Are you a religious man, Philio?" asked Grover Townsend.

"Yes sir, I am. I am a devout Roman Catholic" the young man answered.

"That's highly commendable." said Townsend. "Cy are you religious?"

"The law is my religion. The library is my temple." said Cy.

"That's fine. Sounds like 18th century deism as in Jefferson and Thomas Payne." said Townsend.

"Well...." Cy began, obviously reflecting upon his words. "...that may well be." Cy allowed this to drag out in a vague, hopeful manner.

"I myself am just a plain old Methodist." said Grover.

"My religion is my gun." said Hammersley. Monroe smoothly reached beneath his black suit coat and pulled out a Colt .45 from his shoulder holster. He hefted it lovingly, then slipped it back into the well oiled leather holster. "Standard issue of the U.S. Army since 1911" he added with a tight smile.

"Well, that is fine too." said Grover, with a sort of tolerant disinterest. Monroe's remark began a tough silence. And the four men thought about the matters at hand. Finally, Grover turned to Cy and said: "Why don't you go over to Platteville and have a talk with that old man your friend Ken Starky told you about. Monroe, perhaps you could accompany Mr. Butt?"

Monroe gave Cy a mock look of assessment and said: "I guess I could risk it."

"The heroes go in quest to search out the monster." said Cy with an amused tone.

"What the hell is that?" replied Monroe with a gravelly growl.

" Campbell." replied Cy.

"Oh, just what we need. Canned soup!" sneered Monroe.

Chapter 13
Sunday, October 18, 1953
Platteville, Wis

The day after their meeting with Townsend and Philio, Cy and Hammersley drove over to Platteville to talk with Ken Starky. The editorial offices of Ken's *Other Worlds* magazine were located on a hill-climbing side street lined with old stone business buildings, most of them older than even the oldest structures in Madison. Platteville was in existence for a couple of decades before Madison was ever envisioned. Beneath this city of about 10,000 (if one includes the approximately 5,000 college students of the state college) is a network of long abandoned lead mine tunnels. The local college was for this reason a world renowned mining school.

Stretching out in two lines on either side of the old, narrow street were clusters of business shingles which advertised doctors' offices, lawyers' offices, realtors, title companies, and such. These drab signs contrasted sharply with Ken's flamboyantly painted placard:

"Other Worlds Magazine, Book Store, and Publishers", with its painted images of a quarter moon, Saturn and rings, and a rocket ship spaced evenly beneath the words. As they walked down the street, Cy once again heard Monroe tell that John Dillinger's lawyer's office had been in the upstairs of one of these buildings.

As they stepped up to the door of Ken's building, Cy took note of the blizzard of lecture announcements, concert flyers, cartoons, recipes, photos of famous people (living and dead) all taped on the inside of the windows of the storefront entrance way. Among the faces, Cy saw Albert Einstein, Paracelsus, William Blake, Frank Lloyd Wright, Helen Keller, Emma Goldman, Jesus, Theodore Roosevelt, George Washington, U.S. Grant, and Ernest Hemingway. He could not imagine what system was behind their selection and placement, and had never dared to ask-- out of a fear of hurting Ken's feelings and a reluctance of being snoopy.

They did not readily lay eyes upon Ken, but he had spotted them right away (perhaps he had been watching for their approach through the front windows). As soon as the creaky, belled door opened, Cy heard Ken's voice call out (strangely from above):

"Hey there, glad to see you. What happened to you the other day, Cy? Big meeting with the Attorney General?"

The gnomish Ken descended the steps leading to the loft sleeping quarters and came over to meet his guests. Cy watched the spindly, dwarfish figure approach--with Ken's ever present smile and his typical arm load of books.

"Ken, meet Monroe P. Hammersley of the Madison

Police Department" and the two men shook hands. Both visitors accepted Ken's hospitality of wooden folding chairs. Only Cy accepted a glass of I.W. Harper whiskey (which Ken kept in a drawer just for Cy's occasional visits). Cy proceeded to regale Ken with the mysterious tale of his adventures in Vernon County. And, without missing a beat, without pausing for Ken's reaction, Cy shifted gears and asked about the aliens living in the Earth:

"What was that you were saying about people from outer space living in tunnels under Madison?" asked Cy.

"Under Madison and the rest of the world too." Ken nodded, shielding his face with a coffee cup to thwart Cy's effort to read his expression. Cy watched the stringy mustache wiggle on either side of the cup. "After you left, or were kidnapped I guess, the Prof said he knew where you could access the tunnel in Madison between the two lakes. It was one of those old hotels east of the capitol building, Hotel Grant."

"I know it well." said Cy.

"Well that is one place you can go in Madison to find one of these tunnels." said Ken, decisively. .

"Who built them?" asked Cy.

"Creatures called Derros." Ken said, still shielding his face with the coffee cup.

"What are Derros? And how did you find out about this, assuming it is true?" Cy asked with a bit of a humorous edge to his words.

Ken now removed the cup and responded to Cy by nodding, smiling and digging through a nearby pile of back issues of *Other Worlds* magazine. Finally, he came up with an issue featuring a strange reptile-like creature on the cover. This creature was not terribly different from the entity or vision Cy had seen in the haymow. The creature seemed to be entering a sort of cave, a ray gun in one hand, and dragging a buxom but terrified maiden by the other. She seemed to be casting desperate looks back to a small group of horrified men and women who were watching from a safe distance.

"The Derros are these giant reptile creatures?" asked Cy, cautiously.

"No, they are different. Maybe helpers of the reptiles. A few years ago, *Amazing Stories,* a magazine in Chicago began to run stories allegedly from a guy named Shaver who was saying that there were these mysterious creatures living under the Earth. He called them Derros, and said that they were abducting people and manipulating world events. They were supposed to be aiding these giant reptile people. I laughed the minute I saw the first letter in print. But not long after that I began to get letters like that. So I printed them too. The reaction was phenomenal. People from all over the country began sending me stuff at my magazine as well. The same thing happened to magazines all over the country."

"Are you telling me that this is really true? That you believe it?" asked an incredulous Monroe.

"Well, looks go upstairs and talk to the man who knows." said Ken.

"Really, who?" asked Cy.

"A man named Enoch Clover. An old Negro man. He is at least ninety years old. He was a carpenter, a builder of round barns, all over Wisconsin."

"Round barns?" said Cy, his interest suddenly piqued.

"Yes, but that was years ago. Since I have known him, he has lived in a little room in the back of this building, which I let him have in return for his sweeping, snow shoveling, being an all around handy man. Well, for the past month he had been failing, so I put him upstairs in my own quarters because it is warmer there. He is half dead with cancer. I don't know how he stands the pain. He refuses to go to a doctor. I can't believe I let him talk me into taking him fishing just a few days ago. He could have died on me. Sitting by himself on the river bank." "Fishing?." asked Cy, scratching his chin,. "Loves to fish does he?" said Cy grinning warmly.

"Never seen him ever pick up a pole since I've known him." said Ken. "I dropped him off at the river and went and visited a friend. I just hate to fish. A crashing bore I'm afraid. When I came back Enoch was full of this story about some kind of creature that came up out of the water and spoke with him."

"What kind of creature?" asked Cy.

"Some kind of amphibian creature who came down from the sky and landed in Africa. Enoch was born in Africa. In a place called Dogonland. I looked for it on the map, but it isn't there. I guess it was or is some place in French West Africa. How he got here, I'm not sure. He says he was taken as a child and somehow ended up in the hands of the French. Later on he was taken to the French West Indies. Somehow he ended up in the U.S. South just before the Civil War."

"Hmmmm." Cy scratched his chin further.

"Well, listen Cy. This gets real interesting. Ever since he was taken from his people, he has been guided by the amphibian creatures. Anyway, he tells me how the creatures taught mankind how to work with iron, gave them other skills like language and agriculture. He told me that he had seen them."

"In Africa?"

"Yes, and here in Wisconsin too. In swamps and rivers, I guess. They taught him how to build round barns. "

"Why would they do that? "asked Cy.

"Well, because they are good folks I guess. Although not all of them are." said Ken.

"Not all of them? You mean there are others?"

"Yes, apparently there are different kinds of these creatures. All of them manipulating things behind the scenes. The bad ones are abducting people,...killing people." Ken's words trailed off, fearfully. "Let's go upstairs and see Enoch." Ken added. Ken rose and led his visitors up the steps to the loft.

"What do you think about all this stuff, Ken?" Cy asked as they climbed the stairs, now trying to adopt a more friendly open manner in his interrogation.

"Well, to me it's a story. It's something that might sell magazines. And it does. But at the same time I wouldn't be in this business if I didn't have a yen to see some of these weird stories get proven. Sort of like Charles Fort."

"Who's that?" Cy asked.

"He was a writer. He's been dead for years. But he wrote books about anomalous events--toads falling from the sky, people disappearing from one place and reappearing someplace else, mysterious ships in the sky. His most famous book is *The Book of the Damned.*"

"So he was the writer who inspired you to do all this?" Cy gestured with his whiskey glass at the book shelves below.

"Probably so. But I was a reader of all kinds of books. Even took a number of college courses here, but never graduated. Kind of like you. " Ken chuckled.

"Oh, I've graduated. Any number of times." Cy joining in on the chuckling.

"Speaking of books...Enoch even has a book here about the Dogons. It is in French, fortunately I can read some of it--thanks to the Platteville University and the French courses I took on a lark. It is called *Dieu d'Eau* or *Water God."*

"Water God?" Cy said, reflecting on the words as he said them.

"Amphibians, remember?" said Ken. "Let's go upstairs and talk to Enoch." he added.

The three men now reached the top of the rickety steps from the main floor. They gathered at the side of a bed heaped with quilts and blankets. From the midst of these multi-colored cloths emerged a bald, black head of extraordinary roundness. Cy noticed that Enoch's lips were not particularly large, his face was mostly hairless except for a short beard beneath his chin. The eyes were open and alert, the face seemed wise and friendly. A smell of old man and sickness pervaded the loft. Various bottles of medicine sat on a bedside table.

Enoch looked up at Cy and smiled and said:

"Praise the Lord! Mr. Cy Butt. It is a true pleasure to meet the man Mr. Ken has spoken about so often." And Enoch held up a long, bony, black arm and offered to shake hands with Cy. Which Cy readily did with a smile. "and you have brought a friend." Enoch held out a hand for Monroe, who did shake it with a polite nod and even a smile. Racism was not one of Monroe's numerous faults.

Then Enoch looked up at Ken, and smiled and said:

"I want to thank you again my friend for giving me your own bed. You didn't need to do that." Enoch said in a voice so weak it was almost a gasp.

"You should have let me take you to the hospital Enoch." said Ken, plaintively.

"There would be no point in it. It would only make the doctors richer." said Enoch with the best wry grin he could muster. Both Cy and Ken chuckled.

"I was hoping you could tell Cy here some of the things you told me." said Ken, hopefully.

"About the Nommo, may the Lord praise them, and what they said." said Enoch levelly.

"Yes, that's right." said Cy, hopefully.

"Well, I could hear you speaking as you were down stairs. You basically have got it right, Ken." said Enoch.

While the four men were conversing, Bernard listened. He had followed Monroe's car from Madison, and he had followed the two men as they walked through the twisting streets of Platteville. He also had climbed up a fire escape and found a hiding and listening place above them all. He had a switch blade knife ready at hand--to use on the old blabber mouth down below. He leaned against a sky light and listened to the words drift up to him. However, he was just now beginning to notice problems with his perch. The caulk around the skylight was old and crumbly. It was disintegrating before his eyes. Bernard also noticed that some of the panes he was leaning upon were giving way.

In a horrible moment, Bernard realized that he was

collapsing down through the window and falling towards the bed holding the old man. As he fell, he for a brief, unnerving moment made eye contact with the old man who actually gave him a calm smile.   In a shower of dust, broken glass, caulk, and cobwebs Bernard crashed upon the old black man and his bed. As soon as he realized he was basically unhurt, Bernard swiftly ran the sharp blade over the throat of the old man like slicing into a tomato. Bernard enjoyed the pathetic, yet oddly friendly expression on Enoch's face.   In the next moment, Bernard enjoyed the gurgling sound the blood made as it flowed out of the man's slit throat. Then he quickly scrambled up and ran across the floor of the loft to the stairway. As he ran down the steps he shot a quick glance back to Cy, Ken and Monroe who had fallen to the floor, too stunned to stand up or even speak. However, in another moment Monroe had recovered sufficiently to pull out his Colt .45 pistol and begin blasting a couple of shots in the general direction of their assailant. Some books were rendered to confetti and a plaster of Paris bust of Ben Franklin was exploded to smithereens. Bernard sprang down the steps of the rickety loft stairs, three or four steps at a time. Only after Bernard had made his exit to the street did Cy finally recognize the man who had kidnapped him:

"That's that guy!!!" Cy's bony finger stabbed the air in Bernard's direction.

Monroe moved with surprising vigor from the loft and down the stairs, Cy was in close pursuit.

"Come on, Ken." shouted Cy." We have to get that guy. He's the one who kidnapped me the other day." said Cy.

"I gotta stay here Cy, look what he did." And Ken pointed to the lifeless form of Enoch on the collapsed bed, blood oozing freely from the slash across his throat.

Nevertheless, Cy and Monroe reached the door, leaving Ken behind. By the time they reached the street, Bernard could just be seen as a distant figure rounding the corner, heading right. Monroe blasted a couple more shots at the gangster, much to the shock of shoppers and students in downtown Platteville. With all the effort they could muster they managed to make it up to the corner in time to see Bernard climb into a tan colored DeSoto. They missed the license plate number.

They returned to the bookstore and immediately called the Platteville police station. Within minutes the entire three man force was at the bookstore investigating the murder, as well as the alleged murderer. Quick calls were made to Attorney General Townsend in Madison. Eventually, reports were correlated indicating that the car might have been a car stolen in La Crosse some days ago.

Chapter 14
Monday, October 19, 1953
LaCrosse, Wisconsin

Madeline Marley did not usually go to movies on week days, but her good friend Louise Scovil had been given two free passes which could not be used on the weekends. The fact that the passes were for the theater showing *War of the Worlds* made the event all the more special. Science fiction was one of her atypical delights. It probably went along with her desire to get beyond the boring world of the suburbs around her.

Her homework had been finished before supper, and as she gathered up the supper plates her mother smiled and told her to run along and join her friend. Madeline kissed her Mom and Dad and scampered out of the house to meet Louise a few doors down the winding suburban street. The spindly trees in front of the one story modern houses did not bother her as much at night. It was a pleasant Fall evening and would be a nice walk downtown with Louise. If they had gone to the movies last week, Louise (who was sixteen and had her driver's license) would have been able to drive them. But last week her father's car had been stolen. So far the police had turned up no leads on the missing, tan DeSoto.

As it happened, that very tan DeSoto, stolen on Madeline's street, was resting at the bottom of the Kickapoo River. It had been pushed there off an embankment by Bernard, who had later stolen a car in LaFarge--a green and white, older model Chevrolet. This was the car he sat in now, as he waited around the corner from Madeline. The wire tap he had installed on her family phone had gleaned the information about tonight's trip to the movies. He would cautiously follow the two girls as they went to the show. He would not grab Madeline yet, although he wanted to. The Master specifically had warned him not to do anything until Saturday. And Bernard knew better than enrage the Master.

Once they began their walk downtown, Louise and Madeline began to talk happily about school matters and the movie they were about to see: *War of the Worlds*. Science fiction was one interest that these two girls both shared. For some reason, girls were not supposed to enjoy such films. But Madeline and Louise did. Probably Madeline more than Louise. Madeline thought that Louise basically didn't mind the films, and enjoyed more the chit chat they engaged in coming and going to the theater. Madeline's favorite science fiction films and books were of the type that involved visits to other worlds. She very much enjoyed the Buck Rogers and Flash Gordon serials, even though she knew she was supposed to regard them as childish. She enjoyed the concept of other worlds, other customs, she just knew that she was destined to lead a life of learning and exploration in some other place. Maybe she could become a missionary in Africa, or a school teacher on an Indian reservation out west.

Bernard parked the car in a lot across from the Winnebago Theater, on Main Street. He quietly locked the car and waited until the girls came merrily walking together down the street to the theater. Then he entered the theater, purchased a ticket, and followed the girls at a distance, sitting four rows behind them, but directly behind them. At first he expected two boys to show up out of the darkness and join the two girls for a clandestine date. But, the girls seemed to actually be giving their full attention to the film on the screen. This was not traditional female fare, Bernard realized. This Madeline must be interested in outer space. There might be a way of putting this knowledge to use this weekend. In a few days, Saturday night, to be specific, as according to the info gleaned on the wire tap Madeline would be left alone in the Marley house, babysitting for friends, while everyone else went to the football game.

Chapter 15
Friday, October 23, 1953
Madison, Wis

Philio long remembered the day he found out that Cy Butt was a nudist.

A few days after the old Black man, Enoch Clover, had been murdered, Townsend had instructed Philio to go down to where Cy was then lodging--in a seedy academic apartment house, built of old, dark red brick covered with ivy vines. This venerable establishment, catering to foreign students, was on lower Langdon Street, just up from the Memorial Union. Philio was instructed to be sure to go there before 8 A.M.--in order to be sure that Cy would be passed out in his bed, and therefore not "off on some wild goose chase". But Philio was shocked to find him at 7:54 A.M. not only up and around, but also completely naked.

Cy saw the shock in Philio's eyes and casually said: "Oh, Philio...I should have warned you...I'm a nudist." He then immediately turned about face and headed

111

back into his rooms, saying: "shut the door behind you, I'm having breakfast in the back room."

Cy walked briskly back to a long table in a long back room, surrounded by a bank of windows framed by outside plants. He sat down on a chair at one end of the table and returned to a bowl of some cereal sort of thing, floating around in milk. Hanging by a slender thread over his chair and now his head was a long, Middle Eastern curved blade saber. Philio stood next to the table and gazed with shock at this sword, and the obvious threat it posed to the scrawny life of Cy Butt.

"I see that you are interested in my symbol of death." said Cy, not looking up a bit, his attention directed instead to the morning paper.

"Well, I certainly can't help it." said Philio.

"And that is precisely the idea. Except I am the object of my own message." Cy replied, looking up from the paper with a sly grin. "I find that it focuses my mind mightily." said Cy, who then cut loose with his typical cackle.

"Well, you're the one who knows best how you think." said Philio, cautiously.

"Exactly, and the point of the sword has been focusing my brain on this case of the Master and his cohorts. I'm thinking now about those red cows. " said Cy, pensively lounging one leg over the wooden arm of his chair. Philio stared straight at the floor.

"Red cows?" asked Philio, finally.

"Yes, those red cows I saw in that round barn. There can't be a lot of cows like that." said Cy.

"Maybe they were dyed." said Philio, uncomfortably.

"You're not from the country are you Philio?" asked Cy.

"No Sir. I'm from Green Bay." answered Philio.

"Well, that's a fine town. But the only cows there are in packing plants, hence 'Packers'" Cy cackled. Then he went on for a long time still reading the paper and eating cereal.

"Have a seat there Philio, please." said Cy, not lifting up his eyes from the paper.

Philio sat down. He peered across the table and saw that Cy seemed to be reading agricultural reports in the back pages of the "Wall Street Journal".

After Cy completed his meal he dressed in yet another dismal, thread-bare brown suit (the previous model worn in the Master's cow barn was no doubt at the cleaners). It had been five days since Philio had accompanied Mr. Townsend and Cy Butt to meet with Detective Hammersley in the roadside tavern. In that time, Cy had not been in contact with the Attorney General or the police. It was Philio's assignment today to find Cy and drive him where he wanted to go. Philio did not pretend to understand what was going on with Cy and Grover and Hammersley. He just drove where he was told, did what he was told, and he hoped that a career in State government for many years would be his reward.

Philio's two passenger Nash bumped down Langdon Street, passing the tree-strewn lawns of Fraternity Row. Not so long ago, Philio had lived in one of these frat houses (he sighed as he remembered those carefree days). "Here, left" said Cy, suddenly rousing Philio from his reverie as the reached the corner of Langdon and Park, between the Memorial Union and the University Library. Philio turned left, onto Park Street, and they wheeled past the red brick Gothic, five-story, fortress of

Science Hall. Philio remembered the legend of Cy's practical jokes as they passed Music Hall. Per Cy's instructions they turned right onto University Avenue and headed out to the Agriculture campus. After driving some distance past fields and cow barns, they pulled up next to the enormous Queen Anne mansion of the Dean of Agriculture. Without a word, Cy leaped from the car, and ran up the sidewalk of the imposing residence. Philio followed along behind as quickly as he could.

The door chime could already be heard as Philio began climbing the painted wood steps onto the wide, Victorian porch. A white coated, elderly Black male servant met the two men at the door. Philio half expected a stiff interrogation, which he would have to terminate by flashing his Justice Department credentials. But much to his surprise, the old Black man simply said: "Well, hello again Mr. Butt. The Dean is waiting to meet you in the library." Then he smiled warmly at Cy, and then he ceased smiling and looked at Philio, moving his meticulous gaze up and down the young man's thread bare brown suit.

"It's alright Carlyle. This is Mr. Philio DeGarmo and he's with me." said Cy with a broad smile to Philio.

"Then it's quite alright Mr. Butt. Come on in." and Carlyle held out his arms to the nearby library in a welcoming gesture.

The library was a room with ceiling to floor book shelves, interrupted only by a couple of windows and the entry door. The shelves were a dark, red Mahogany color, and were more eye catching than the armies of scholarly volumes contained within. In the center of the room was a long library table, with a few chairs spaced regularly along its sides. One large arm chair sat at the head of the table, and in this chair sat an elderly, short, pot-bellied, man with wisps of white hair streaking across his freckled scalp. He was wearing rimless spectacles. And with a warm broad southern accent that Philio could not quite identify, but which Cy later told him was Virginia Tidewater mixed with Kentucky bourbon with a sprig of Harvard yard : "Greetings, Cy! It's been quite a while since you last visited here. Why don't you and your friend sit here near me and tell me about your errand?"

Cy and Philio sat at either side of the man at the end of the table.

"Cy, as usual, you are forgetting your manners. Why don't you introduce me to your friend?

"Oh, yes, Dean Parker, this is Philio DeGarmo, an assistant to the attorney general."

"Well, what are you two researching today?"

"Cows and barns, Dean."

"What kind of cows, Cy?"

"Red ones.

"What kind of barns?"

"Round ones."

"I think I need a bit more information than that Cy."

Cy looked over at Philio, who was stunned to see that his permission was being asked for anything by Cy. Philio nodded earnestly to Cy, giving the Justice Department's permission to include this bespectacled figure in on the investigation. And Cy unfolded an extremely edited version of the events that Philio had been thoroughly briefly on.

When Cy finished, Dean Parker tapped the tips of his fingers together for a long time, saying nothing.

Finally he said just two words: "Vernon County". Then without a word, the Dean rose, and like a busy elf he scurried over to the library ladder on wheels and pushed it over to a particular location. Then he climbed up two or three steps and pulled a large, thick book from a shelf. Philio stood immediately to help the Dean with the book. Philio took a heavy book in his hands and looked at the title on the cover: *Illustrated Guide to Dairy Cattle Breeds--Worldwide*

"Thank you Mr. DeGarmo." said the Dean without looking away from the shelves. The Dean then picked another, slimmer volume. The Dean was able to handle this volume effectively himself as he climbed down the ladder. The Dean then led the way back to the table.

"Place your volume in front of Mr. Butt, would you Mr. DeGarmo." said the Dean, seemingly engrossed in paging through the smaller book, the title of which Philio could see was *Round Barns of Wisconsin.*

The Dean stood next to Cy as he leafed through the small book, saying in an offhand manner: "Vernon County, your home county I understand, contains more round barns than any other county in Wisconsin, perhaps the United States. There were a couple of renowned builders of these structures there--"

"One of them named Enoch Clover?" asked Cy.

"Yes,. as a matter of fact that is one of the names I see listed. He would be quite elderly, well into his nineties. He might even be deceased."

"He is now." said Cy with a sarcastic tone."

"Nevertheless," the Dean droned on. "Round barns do serve a number of important functions, feed can be tossed down from the hay mow to the center facilitating easier feeding than in a box-like structure. The movement of the animals through the structure is easier. However, the farmer is limited in his space, adding an addition to a round structure is awkward. And they are more expensive to build, requiring a considerable amount of technical ability. With the ever growing size of dairy herds they are probably a footnote in dairy history. Corporate farms don't like round barns. As Frank Lloyd Wright said the box is a fascist symbol. The round barns are a symbol of the doomed family farm. Nevertheless, they are beautiful, even sublime, and I try to stop and examine them every chance I get. If you were confined in a round barn in Wisconsin, its photograph is almost certainly in this book. Why don't you take a look."

So saying the Dean handed the book to Cy, who began to page through it dubiously:

"The barn I was in was definitely round, but you say there are lots of them up there."

"Yes there are, Cy."

"I don't know Dean, round is round. I was sort of pinning my hopes on those red cows I saw."

"Well, let's consult this other book." and with that the Dean opened an enormous, hardcover, brown suede book replete with full color portraits of hundreds of dairy cows. After a couple of minutes of page turning, Cy's eyes lit upon a particular breed--Red Norwegian Pole Cows.

"There they are!" Cy said triumphantly.

"Hmmmmm. Quite rare, in this country at least." said the Dean.

Philio looked at the glossy photo of a strikingly red animal. So red that it almost looked like somebody had painted the stolid beast as a joke. However, the color was clearly natural, and was not marred by so much as one white spot, from back to hoof, from nose to tail.

"So, you are looking for Norwegian Pole Cows kept in a round barn. That shouldn't be too hard. Let me call some people. Beginning with your home county of Vernon."

The Dean left the room, presumably to use a phone. Cy and Philio sat together at the library table. An awkward silence ensued. Cy paged through the book on dairy cows with the concentration of a dairy expert about to buy a herd. Finally, Philio could stand it no more and had to ask:

"Tell me Cy. How is it that you know this man so well. You've taken all kinds of courses at the University I know, but certainly never agricultural classes, have you?"

"Well, as it turns out Philio, old man, I *have* taken classes in agriculture from this very man. Not any that ever helped me in any field of endeavor, except maybe bar lectures, but still they were courses and I did pass them. I've taken courses here for many, many years." Cy said, with a satisfied grin.

The Dean came back into the room. In his hand was a small slip of paper.

He handed it to Cy, much to Philio's annoyance. He craned his neck to see a rural address in Vernon County.

"I was right." the Dean grinned happily. "It is in Vernon County. The only herd of Norwegian Pole Cows kept in a round barn in the state. And, despite what I said about corporate farms not liking round barns, strangely enough, this herd is owned by a corporation. A Swiss corporation."

"Well, a nugget of research like that must be toasted with a drink!!! But if I recall Dean, you don't indulge." said Cy, pulling out his hip flask.

"Indeed, I do not Cy. That you well know." said the Dean, with a determined set of jaw. "And if you had been a bit more temperate yourself, you might be the Attorney General yourself, instead of doing secret research for one."

"Perhaps, Dean. Perhaps. But I would have to run on the Populist Party ticket like by grandpa did, and they don't get too many votes these days. " said Cy, laughing.

"Indeed they don't Cy" now laughing. "My father, as you know, was once a Populist State Senator. But you aren't going to deflect me that easily, young man.

Philio snickered inwardly at the elderly Dean calling Cy a young man.

"You could still amount to something you know. What a law professor you would have made. You're not even fifty are you? You've got the common touch, a definite flair and doggedness for law work, you could be an elected official." said the Dean, an earnest expression on his face.

"But could I be happy?" asked Cy, a sincere look on his face.

"Are you really happy now?" asked the Dean, firmly.

"Yessir. I am." said Cy.

Later, Same Day...

Philio dutifully drove Cy up to the Hotel Grant on the east side of the capitol building. He asked no questions as Cy led the way into the hotel lobby, and followed him as he walked grandly over to the elevator. This once elegant hostelry now catered to male transients and drifters. Cy gave a cautious look at the desk clerk who was distracted by a discussion about the baseball game being broadcast on the radio. The clerk's southern Illinois twang clashed sharply with an Irish taxi driver who leaned against desk. Cy punched the button for the second floor and when the ancient car trundled to a halt at its destination, without a word, Cy led Philio to the back staircase. They walked to the basement and walked to the furnace room. There, on the back wall was an old, soot covered iron door. Cy tried to open it. But it wouldn't budge.

"Maybe it's locked, Cy." said Philio.

"The Prof said it wouldn't be. Said it is just hard to open. Give a pull on the handle." said Cy excitedly.

Philio pulled on the filthy door with all his strength, and at first was certain it was either locked or welded shut. But suddenly, it budged a bit. Both men pulled on the door, and finally with a sharp metallic groan it gave way. After the door was opened, the two men found themselves facing a black void. Philio groped the walls for a light switch, without success. He was startled to see a small metal flashlight erupt into brilliance in the hands of Cy Butt.

"I carried this with me just for this expedition." Cy said with some satisfaction.

Before them was a narrow concrete staircase which they followed in a number of switchbacks until they reached what appeared to be a subbasement. Their progress came up against another iron door. From his pocket this time, Cy produced an enormous iron key, obviously of some age.

"Where did you get that?" Philio asked.

"I cannot and will not tell you." said Cy, firmly. "I gave my word as a gentleman and a scholar."

"Well, then I suspect that I know who gave it to you." said Philio.

"I suspect you do." said Cy.

Cy inserted the key into the door. The lock appeared to have been oiled and maintained, for it opened easily. When the door was opened they found themselves entering a long corridor which stretched off into the unlit darkness as far as the flashlight would project. Cy resolutely turned to the right and led the way--almost not looking back at Philio at all.

The corridor was lined with stone, obviously of some age. Philio somehow came to the conclusion--despite the darkness--that they were moving downwards, perhaps toward one of the lakes. From time to time they passed entranceways in the stone walls leading to other corridors. Cy ignored these other corridors, however, and continued to lead Philio doggedly on. After walking for an indeterminate amount of time in the damp darkness, they came up against another door. This time they faced an old wooden door. This they tried and found it unlocked. They entered a strange sloping porch, obviously overlooking Lake Monona. They found no one there. They crossed the porch and opened another old wooden door. They entered an enormous, curving stone staircase, climbing down the steps cautiously. From somewhere below them distant voices seemed to echo.

The staircase ended at a large garage. Several cars and an old pickup truck were parked within. Three men could be seen at the far end of the garage engaged in an animated conversation. Cy instantly recognized the Master, Bernard and Ned Lein.

"Well at least I killed the old guy." whined Bernard.

"I know Bernard, but it was messy." said the Master.

Cy motioned for Philio to join him in the tarp covered box of the pickup truck. Slowly, quietly, they climbed into the back of the truck and waited. After a bit, Cy began to feel a wet, furry object grazing against his face. He carefully flicked on his flashlight. Cy was startled to see the ram's head from the other night, still redolent of urine. Philio was out and out horrified. He could not help but emit a muffled yelp.

"What was that?" said Bernard.

"What was what?" asked Ned.

"I heard something too." said the Master. "I think there is somebody else here."

Suddenly, footsteps could be heard coming down the stone stair case.

"Master, Master," said a voice which Cy and Philio recognized as the distinctive southern Illinois crackle of the desk clerk of the Hotel Grant. "That lawyer Cy Butt has found the secret corridor. I think he is probably down here right now! He is probably bringing the police with him."

Not quite, thought Philio, ruefully.

The Master announced his plan: "We've got to get out of here immediately, and we can't trust the streets. This place might be surrounded. Come on, all of you, let's go below and get into the speed boat and escape across the lake. "

In a few moments, Cy and Philio heard another door open and close indicating that the men had left the garage. They exited the back of the truck. They looked about the garage for a door which might lead to a lower area accessing the lake. When they finally found it, they could already hear a high powered motor boat roaring into action beneath them. They opened the door to a staircase leading to an indoor boat slip. Quickly they descended the stairs only to see a fast motor boat containing the Master, Bernard, Ned and the desk clerk speeding across the choppy waters of Lake Monona. Even if they had a phone in their very hands, a call to the police would not be able to intercept the men before they reached the other side.

Indeed, when Cy and Philio finally did reach a phone and called Monroe P. Hammersley, the boat was being abandoned on the other side of the lake near a garage rented for just such an emergency. Four men, led by a bulky bald headed man in gray, were seen climbing into a vehicle and speeding out of the garage with squealing tires. Neighbors had no idea who the men were or who rented the garage. Nobody got a license plate or even a definite direction of travel.

Later that night in Madison, Professor Alterweise was almost asphyxiated by a mysterious gas leak in his apartment. Only the sudden visit by Red, the bartender at Nino's Bar, saved the day. Red was delivering a hamburger and smelled gas the moment he tried the unlocked door. He was smart enough to not turn on the lights, thereby risking a spark. He correctly guessed that the Prof would be in his usual alcove asleep, so Red dragged the short, gasping body out into the cool night air.

Chapter 16
Saturday, October 24, 1953
La Crosse, Wis.

After some convincing, Monroe P. Hammersley had agreed to ride with Cy Butt and Philio DeGarmo to Vernon County and LaCrosse County to investigate the leads that Cy had uncovered. There was one Dane County homicide and a Grant County homicide that Monroe would have loved to be investigating at the crime scenes, rather than go on this goose chase. However, the fact that the day was Saturday probably played a role in his thinking. What could possibly happen on a Saturday?

Cy also hated to leave town while his friend the Prof was so dangerously ill as a result of what must have been a bungled murder attempt. Nevertheless, he felt that things were coming to a head in this investigation and weekend or no he implored his two associates to come with him to LaCrosse.

Philio sat alone in the front, driving Monroe's powerful, black-colored, 1952 Buick. Cy and Monroe sat in the back seat. Cy dozed and made wise cracks.

Monroe droned on, making sarcastic, sometimes obscene remarks about rural life:

"And another damned thing about these farms....the smell! Haven't any of these people ever heard of disinfectant? Why don't they spray a little Lysol or Pine sol around these places?" Monroe asked, directed at nobody in particular.

Cy, who for some reason, had taken on the role of spokesperson for Rural America since the ride began, merely said: "I think that would harm the animals, Monroe. There's some pretty strong juice in those disinfectants you know."

"Well then screw 'em!" Monroe growled.

In such a manner, the conversation rolled along as the Buick passed the hillsides and crossed the streams of the Kickapoo Valley. They headed north, up to LaFarge, and finally left the valley on a narrow gravel road, dust a'flying behind them. Philio pressed down the pedal of the powerful engine to climb a steep, twisting, tree hugged road. At the end of the road they found themselves in the driveway of a seemingly abandoned ridgetop farm. The dung-spattered barnyard showed signs of recent use, but there was not a cow to be seen. Most importantly, the barn itself was round.

The trio entered the barn, still aromatic of the recent bovine occupants, and as soon as he saw the top of the barn, with its round shape, Cy almost passed out. It was the very place where he had been held prisoner by the Master and his minions. The three men climbed onto the elevator leading to the haymow. Cy instructed Philio in its operation, and soon the three of them were rising up into the haymow. As soon as they reached this upper story, Cy noticed the round blood spot on the floor where the ram's head had been. He also noticed certain non blood dribbles which seemed to leave an acrid smell. He did not enlighten his companions as to their origin.

Suddenly from below, they heard a man's voice:

"Hey, who's up there?" said a gruff voice. "Come on down here, whoever you are. I got a gun."

Monroe confidently patted a bulge in his suit coat pocket.

Philio again pulleyed the three men back to the ground floor of the barn.

Cy was genuinely floored to meet again Thomas Torgerson, Sr., the father of his traffic court client of a few days earlier (although it seemed like a lifetime, or two).

"Well, Mr. Butt!" said Torgerson, obviously quite surprised and no longer unfriendly. No gun seemed evident.

"Good afternoon Mr. Torgerson. Do you own this farm?" asked Cy.

"No Mr. Butt. I rent some of the crop land. And a day or so ago they took all those strange red cows away and told me they were leaving for good." said Torgerson.

Cy was able to quickly ascertain that the farm had recently been rented to an unknown Swiss corporation. The owner was the estate of an old woman who died three years ago, managed by a La Crosse law firm. It was the La Crosse law firm of the mysterious blond haired lawyer Cy had met in court, and met later upstairs in the haymow during the ceremony.

Cy implied to Torgerson that his two companions were interested in the farm for an investment.

"Well, the barn is a little strange, but it works well."

said Torgerson. "A little old fashioned though. You gents sure don't look like farmers though."

"Well, we aren't." said Cy, affably. "Just investors. Thanks for the information Mr. Torgerson. And please say hello to Tommy and your wife for me.., please." said Cy, with a sort of heartfelt lilt to his voice at the end.

By fortunate chance, the blond lawyer was in his office on Saturday afternoon. That fact alone seemed to make Monroe suspicious for some reason.

"No lawyer is ever up to any good on a Saturday afternoon," he growled confidentially to both of them. After an uncomfortable wait in a tiny inner hallway, chaperoned by a skinny, dour, ageless, hair-in-bun woman dressed in black, the trio was ushered into a huge corner, third story office, overlooking La Crosse's Main Street. There was a bank on the first floor. Through the enormous picture windows, the Mississippi River was viewable some blocks to the west. The noise of the throngs of trucks, cars, and pedestrians below was almost undetectable. Sound proofed, thought Philio.

Monroe led the way to the desk of the lawyer, his Madison police badge in hand. Cy and Philio walked behind Monroe, side by side. Wedge-formation, thought Cy

The lawyer was a delightful, smiling, blond haired, ruddy-cheeked man who stood and agreeably held out his hand in welcome.

"Have a seat gentlemen." he gestured to the three, armless, dark, wooden chairs, already lined up in front of the ultra modernistic, curved desk of hand crafted blond colored wood, glass covered, Swedish look.

Despite his superficial affability, the lawyer was none too forthcoming with information. He sat in his comfortable desk chair, rocking back and forth, bouncing the tips of his fingers together over and over, smiling and first turning his attention to Cy:

"Mr. Butt. Your reputation precedes you of course. We did not exactly get the opportunity to meet the other day in court in Viroqua. Much to my great disappointment."

"It almost seems like we have met elsewhere too." said Cy, giving a slight edge to his words.

"I just have no information that would be of use to you gentlemen that I am in any position to reveal." the blond haired lawyer suddenly said, the afternoon light glinting off his reading glasses.

"How do you know what will be of use to us if you don't know what we want?" asked Cy, with a light-hearted twang.

Monroe gave Cy a silencing side glance: "You have acted as a rental agent, and as such are under obligation to assist the police investigating crimes committed by your renter, perhaps on your property." he said, again holding out the police badge.

After a period of silence, during which time the smile disappeared from the lawyer's face, the lawyer finally said: "What kind of crimes would these be?"

"I'm investigating at least one murder. Grant County is investigating another." said Monroe firmly.

"Did these murders take place on the property being rented by my client?" asked the lawyer.

"No they did not." answered Monroe.

"Then how is my client involved?" the lawyer asked.

"We are not sure. In fact, who is your client?" asked

Monroe.

"I rented that farm for a corporation from Switzerland. It is strictly an agricultural investment for them. Show cattle such as the Norwegian Red Pole cows can bring in quite a bit of money at dairy shows here and in Europe. " the lawyer pronounced expansively.

"Do you have the names of the officers of that corporation?" asked Monroe.

"Yes." said the lawyer, now looking back at Monroe, levelly, unsmilingly, silently.

"Would you mind giving us the names?" asked Monroe.

"Do you have a warrant or subpoena?" asked the lawyer.

"I could get one." said Monroe.

"On a Saturday afternoon?" asked the lawyer.

"We got pull.' said Monroe.

"Yes, I know you do." said the lawyer, looking at Cy, grinning in a toothy manner which actually made Cy rather uncomfortable.

Gradually, the grizzled demeanor of Monroe P. Hammersly, and the caustic wise cracks of Cy Butt wore down the blond lawyer's resistance. A file, already on the desk was opened, and New York and Zurich addresses for the mysterious corporation were copied down. The lawyer called in the sour receptionist, handed her the slip of paper with the information, saying: "Give this to these gentlemen and show them out please, Miss Carstairs."

Monroe accepted the slip of paper and responded to the woman as she handed him the same paper with a smile every bit as evil and fulsome as that of the lawyer. "Thanks for your time." he growled after the smile.

"Let's go gents."

Once they reached the street, Cy suggested they go to a nearby bar, and both men readily agreed.

Finnish Mike's was a an obscure, greasy windowed establishment not far from the docks. Philio assumed that Cy was well-known there, and he was correct. Philio was also shocked to see a large framed painting behind the bar which quite obviously depicted the face of Karl Marx.

"Yes, Philio, that's just who you think it is. Mike is a Red, a lot of Finns are. Unless you want people here to think you are with HUAC or FBI just ignore it. " said Cy, quietly as the three men strolled past the mostly empty tables, and up to the entirely empty bar, manned by a tall, sharp-eyed, gangly figure, who had begun motioning for them to sit on the stools before him.

"Well, Cy Butt, as I live and breathe." said the bartender with a distinctly Finnish accent.

"Mike these are some friends of mine from Madison. Can we ask you some questions?" asked Cy.

The tables immediately emptied and the men sitting there left the room. Cy, Philio, and Monroe were now alone with the bartender.

"Sure Cy. Any friend of yours is a friend of the people. I assume." said the bartender looking Monroe P. Hammersley in the eye. Monroe responded by taking a long drag on his Old Gold and gazing down the empty bar in feigned boredom.

"Well, I wouldn't go quite that far Mike. I have an awful lot of friends, you know. Set us up Mike. I'll have-
-

"I.W.Harper whisky. No ice. I remember Cy. What

can I get you two gentlemen."

"Well, I shouldn't do this...this early in the day." droned Monroe.

"It's the weekend, Monroe." said Cy.

"I'll have a glass of gin. Just plain gin." said Monroe with determination.

"Beer" said Philio. "Old Style as long as we are in La Crosse."

"Mike what do you know about that lawyer up the street?" asked Cy.

"The town is full of lawyers Cy. You wanna narrow it down a little."

Cy described their encounter--being careful to be obscure about their quest. Monroe's vicious side glances made sure of that. Philio gazed at his own reflection in the behind the bar mirror--rehearsing his explanation to Grover W. Townsend of this side trip.

When Mike finally understood who they meant he opened up a bit. That particular lawyer was not, as Mike would say, "a friend of the people". Mike had long suspected him of being involved in all kinds of mischievousness. High level bribes, looting of estates, money laundering (perhaps for the Nazis), and other such activities were just some of the crimes Mike had long suspected of the lawyer. He apparently had attended Yale University, and belonged to some kind of secret society on that campus:

"Skull and Crossbones." said Mike.

"Skull and Bones." corrected Cy.

"Oh, I should have figured youda heard about it, Cy."

Chapter 17
La Crosse, Wis.
4:44 P.M.

The trio exited Finnish Mike's bar, got into Monroe's huge black Buick, and drove up Main Street, with no particular plan of action in mind. Cy and Monroe sat together sullenly in the back seat, while Philio drove, alone in the front. Cy casually let his eyes follow a field of vision bouncing from shop window to shop window. Suddenly, as they passed the huge bank building on the corner, where the office of the sinister blond lawyer was found, Cy spotted Bernard standing in an alley next to the bank building. Cy recognized him immediately.

"Pull over, pull over, here, Philio! There's the guy who hijacked me!" Philio managed to find a parking spot up the block a ways. Cy turned around and craned his neck, keeping his eyes on Bernard.

"I'll get out and follow him." said Cy.

"Here, Cy. Take that special small walkie-talkie with the ear piece that Grover let me borrow. He's got a lot of experimental equipment. Just stick the box in your coat pocket and people will think it's some kind of hearing aid." said Monroe, who was already installing the device into Cy's coat.

"Thanks Monroe. You have one too?" asked Cy.

"Yes, I've got the regular Army Surplus walkie talkie which I'll use here in the car." said Monroe.

"Should we call the La Crosse police department and get them to help us?" asked Philio.

"And tell them what? We are just following some guys?" asked Monroe with a sneer.

"Ok, I understand." said Philio.

"Alright, Gents. Think I'll do a little gum shoe work." said Cy, who exited the car and walked down the other side of the street from Bernard. Bernard was slowly, casually walking down the street, probably looking about to see if he was being followed. So, Cy studied his quarry in the reflection of a huge department store window. Suddenly Bernard seemed to make up his mind and quickly entered the door leading to the offices above the bank.

Cy quickly did an about face and crossed the street, jay-walking with the response of a couple of horn hoots. He reached the other sidewalk and swiftly entered the stairway door. Cy took a chance and walked as quickly but quietly as he could up to the third floor. He walked carefully past the plate glass door of the suite of the blond lawyer. Sure enough, there was Bernard, talking earnestly with the prim and proper receptionist. She seemed as equally unimpressed with Bernard as she had been with Cy and his friends. Cy walked a few doors down the hall until he found a door marked 'Custodian", which he tried, and found unlocked. Cy wedged his way in amidst the brooms, mops, and floor polish. He was able to keep the door propped open so that he could study the lawyer's office door through the crack. He then radioed Monroe and reported his location.

"Keep an eye on him, Cy. We'll find a place to park. " Monroe broadcast over the ear piece.

Cy stayed in the increasingly stuffy closet. Aware of the time--his watch read close to five in the afternoon--he began to fear that a night janitor would come lumbering down the hall. Most of the other offices on the floor seemed to be empty. He wondered what Bernard could be talking about in there with the lawyer. Suddenly, the door of the lawyer's office opened, and Bernard exited with the lawyer escorting him to the door--definitely more chummy treatment than Cy and his two friends received. The lawyer said:

"I know HE is very appreciative of the work you do for him."

"Well, just as long as I get paid." said Bernard, in a somewhat sarcastic manner.

"Yes, of course, I almost forgot. " said the lawyer, who pulled a white envelope out of his coat pocket and handed it to Bernard. "Perhaps I'll see you later," the lawyer added.

"Sure thing." said Bernard, and he then just walked away, back down the stairway. The lawyer watched Bernard for a moment, then went back into his office. Cy waited until the lawyer was back in the office. Cy left the closet, and scurried back quickly down the hallway, and began to slowly, quietly descend the stairway. From above he could see Bernard leave the building at the bottom of the stairs. Cy quickly radioed this news to Monroe and continued to follow.

The streets were already filling up with crowds of revelers anticipating the evening's football game at the college. Homecoming for La Crosse State College was a big deal. Cy had been among the partiers here over the years. Gaily dressed students, alumni, and townsfolk were spreading a festive mood in the streets. But today Cy Butt was ignoring the cheerful atmosphere. He was keeping his eyes on Bernard who was walking ahead of him, moving east on Main Street. Cy knew that it was pointless to stop at Monroe's car and notify his two friends. They could not follow Bernard with the car, and in the time he took doing that he would no doubt lose his man. Also, three men following would attract more attention than just one man. Cy was even reluctant to use the radio device to contact Monroe, as such a scene might attract unneeded attention here on the open street. Cy would just have to radio Monroe when a safe opportunity presented itself.

Cy looked over at the Buick, parked across the street from the sidewalk he was traversing. But he could not get the attention of either Monroe or Philio. Bernard walked swiftly up Main Street, and then crossed Main Street at the 5th Avenue intersection. Cy carefully sauntered along, blending into the crowd as much as possible, glad for the approach of evening. Bernard then crossed 5th Avenue at the Hoeschler Drug Store, and continued east on Main. Cy followed onward. Finally, Cy knew he was getting so far from Monroe's Buick that he ducked into a doorway and radioed a message down the street:

"Why don't you guys start driving up Main Street? I'm next to the Hoeschler Drug store and he is walking east." Cy said into the device, as subtly as possible

"Do you want us to pick you up?" came Monroe's gravely reply.

"No, just drive up the street, past 5th Avenue. Go around the block if you must." said Cy, this time his speaking to an unseen listener attracted the attention of some rowdy college students, who laughed and pointed at him, thinking him drunk. On some other occasion you would be right , kids. But not tonight. Cy laughed and played along with the game, and the kids passed by. Bernard farther up the street did not seem to notice the disturbance. Cy resumed his walking tour, several yards behind Bernard.

Suddenly, Bernard turned and entered a parking lot. Cy halted and bowed his head as if studying a shop window. Bernard then climbed into a green and white, older model Chevy. There was already another occupant in the front seat--none other than the old, toothless farmer of the cow barn some days ago. Cy radioed to Monroe to head to this spot as quickly as possible.

6:30 P.M

Madeline Marley helped her mother with the dinnertime dishes and straightened up the living room in anticipation of the arrival of Mr. and Mrs. Arvid Magnussen with their year and a half old baby daughter, Theresa. While the Marleys did not have television, they did have a good console radio. Moreover, Madeline had selected a number of books and magazines to read during the evening. Football and sports were not her favorite subjects, so she would be one of the few people in LaCrosse not following the game on the radio. Most of the radios along her winding suburban street would be tuned to the shouts and excitement of the football match.

Pops had told Madeline that Professor Magnussen was delighted with the idea of Madeline babysitting their daughter. They were particularly protective parents, and Pops made sure to tell Madeline that the Magnussens would not trust just anybody to take care of Theresa. Chip was going along with his folks to the game, which relieved Madeline because she was afraid that his noisy games and cap pistols would upset the baby. Now, there would be no possible disturbances Madeline resolved. Just a quiet evening looking at National Geographic magazines and day dreaming about some of those long trips she wanted to take some day.

6:35 P.M.

Philio almost lost the green and white Chevy a number of times. Cy made a mental note to inform Grover that the kid needed a course in on road surveillance. Nevertheless, they tailed the car all the way to Losey Boulevard, where it made a right turn and headed south. The flow of traffic was in the opposite direction, as people were now heading in droves to the campus and the football game. Monroe pronounced that the car was probably headed out of town.

"I don't think so Monroe. I think they are up to something big here tonight. Something involving a girl," said Cy. Monroe responded with silence.

Suddenly, near the Trane Company plant, the Chevy turned into a roadside hamburger stand. Monroe had

Philio drive on down Losey and turn around. They next parked behind a gas station in such a way that they had a view of the Chevy. Bernard got out of the car and entered the hamburger stand. He returned to the car with a sack and two coffees.

6:55 P.M.

Professor Marley himself made a circuit of the house, checking each outside door, making sure they were both locked. The Magnussens had arrived a bit late and as it was they were probably going to be late for the kick off of the football game. However, Norman Marley was glad he had taken that extra precaution with the doors. If anything happened to poor , tiny Theresa, the Marleys would never forgive themselves. They were all in a festive mood as they all climbed into the Marley family vehicle--a late model Oldsmobile with more than enough room for five people--unlike the small roadster driven by the young Magnussens.

Madeline watched her family drive down the dark street and walked over to the crib containing Theresa, she shook one of the little mobiles above the baby's head and the baby responded with a delighted squeal. Then Madeline sat down and picked up the *National Geographic* magazine, idly drifting her eyes over the photos.

7:01 P.M.

Bernard and Ned sat in their Chevy, parked at the new hamburger stand called McDonald's near the Trane factory on Losey Boulevard for almost a half hour, munching on sandwiches and drinking coffee. All the while, Cy, Monroe, and Philio watched the pair from the Buick. Finally, the Chevy pulled out onto Losey and headed north. Monroe ordered Philio to follow at a safe distance. After a few blocks, the Chevy made a right turn into one of the newly built subdivisions. Philio followed. However, suddenly, the Chevy made a U turn in the street and came to a halt parked next to the other side of the street. Monroe was certain that they had been spotted and he told Philio to drive on past, make a right and go around the block. Cy watched out the back window and saw Bernard exit the Chevy.

"Let me out here and I'll stay with the Chevy. " he said.

"Okay Cy, but you be careful. You want a gun?" asked Monroe.

"Would you trust me with a gun?" laughed Cy.

"No, I guess not. Just keep us posted on that radio." Monroe growled. And Cy quickly exited the car. He silently crossed the dark street, and entered the vacant lot next to the parked Chevy. From a distance, he could see Bernard disappear down one of the winding streets of the subdivision.

The vacant lot next to the Chevy would in fifteen years be the site of the new La Crosse Central High School. But on this chilly night in 1953 it was grown up with trees and huge clumps of sand hills dotted with sumac and hemp. Using this vegetation as a screen, Cy made his way to the Chevy with cat-like stealth. He finally got even with the front windows of the vehicle and stared in. Much to his surprise, behind the wheel he saw not the grizzled old farmer he had seen in the barn, but the plump face of an elderly woman. Strangely enough, she was wearing the farmer's clothing. Suddenly, the figure in the front seat bent over to adjust the radio dial. Cy noticed with a mixture of fascination and queasiness that the woman's face seemed to sag forward, as if it were just hanging loose on the head. Then Cy realized that it was in fact a mask of some sort, being worn by the farmer. He marveled at the lifelike nature of the mask, even down to the fringe of gray hair covering the shoulders and ears. With those ears covered like that and with the radio dial a focus of attention, Cy Butt could think of no better moment than this one to climb into the trunk of the Chevy. Fortunately, it was one of those trunks opened not by a key, but simply with a latch. Carefully, Cy opened the latch and lifted the trunk lid enough to squeeze himself in. Once in the trunk he listened for a sudden opening car door as an indication that he had been seen. But all Cy heard was the noises of the football game on the radio.

7:15 P.M.

Bernard tried both outside doors on the house, and he found them locked. Annoyed, he next looked at the basement windows and here he was lucky. The basement window was of the type that open inward with a hinge at the top. It was unlocked. Bernard knew that people often forget to lock their basement windows. Bernard slid his weasely form through the window and soundlessly slipped down to the floor of the basement. He crossed over to the basement stairs and carefully, quietly crept up the stairs. He turned the knob at the top of the stairs, opened the door a crack and listened. All he heard was a radio playing classical music.

He opened the door all the way and found himself in the central hallway of the one story house. He walked slowly down the hallway, heading for the living room. He peeked around the corner and saw Madeline Marley sitting in a rocking chair reading a magazine. A baby crib sat next to her. The baby was of no interest to Bernard, although he knew people who would pay him good money for a snatched baby. But that is not what the Master wanted. He wanted the girl and he would get her. All Bernard had to do was to rush quickly into the room, inject her with the powerful drug given to him for this purpose and then walk her back to the waiting car. The drug would not knock her out. She would still be able to walk, but she would have no resistance and be in a complete daze. Bernard reached into his coat pocket and took out the syringe.

Then he rushed into the room, syringe in hand. He almost made it to the girl in the chair before she noticed him. But when he was about four feet from her, she raised her face from the magazine, saw the intruder with a hypodermic syringe in hand and screamed. Neighbors reported hearing a scream, but they wrote it off to a radio play or to fans listening to the football game. Madeline immediately sprang out of her chair and reached the door. Then she remembered the baby, and she could not leave the house without grabbing the baby from this evil intruder who so obviously had bad intentions on his mind. So Madeline turned around, ran past Bernard and headed for the crib. In a moment, Bernard was on her. Madeline fought back by grabbing the metal and plastic mobile over the crib and lashing it fiercely across Bernard's face, nearly succeeding in breaking his nose. She did make several cuts on his face, and the police reported a considerable amount of blood on the floor when they arrived later in the evening.

Nevertheless, Bernard overpowered Madeline and jabbed her with the needle. While she did not collapse in a heap, she did slump against his body. He carefully deposited her semi conscious body in the nearby rocking chair and he went to the family phone, where he removed the phone tap which he had installed some time earlier.

Then he walked her to the door which he opened. He steered her out the door and he carefully closed and locked the door behind them. With his arm behind the dazed girl, Bernard headed back up the dark street to the waiting car. A neighbor did notice the couple walking up the street. He saw them get in the car and saw the car leave, turning south on Losey Boulevard. But he concluded that the couple had been engaging in early Homecoming partying.

7:30 P.M.

Cy listened attentively to the noises in the car from the moment the door opened and somebody entered. Soon he realized that it was two somebodys, and that one of them was Bernard. The other one, a girl, probably the girl he had heard them discuss at the riverside bar. This particular girl was named Madeline:

"Now Madeline, honey, lift your head up. Don't throw up in the car or else we'll have to steal another one (laughs uproariously)." said Bernard.

"Which way do we go?" asked Ned Lein.

"Just go down Losey, then turn south onto Highway 14. We go off the road up in the hills." Bernard replied.

Cy managed to make radio contact with Monroe in the Buick:

"Turn south onto Losey, then go south on Highway 14. They got a girl in the car with them." Cy whispered, hoping that the noise of the ball game would drown out his voice.

"We are turning south onto Losey. I think we have sight of you. Are you in the car?" Monroe asked.

"I'm in the trunk." said Cy.

"So you can't see outside?" asked Monroe.

"I can make out the street behind us somewhat through a hole in the trunk. It looks like we are still on Losey. We are just passing the hamburger stand now." said Cy.

"Then you are ahead of us a ways." said Monroe. "Step on it Philio." Cy heard Monroe growl over the head phones.

"Should you stop and get the LaCrosse police to help you?" asked Cy.

"We can't take the time." said Monroe. "We could completely lose track of you. Hopefully we will catch up to them by the time they stop and I can get out and cover them with my gun."

In a couple of minutes Cy noticed a sudden turn to the left:

"We are turning onto Highway 14, going past the bowling alley." he said.

"I think we see you up ahead." said Monroe.

The sounds of the ballgame still echoed from the front part of the vehicle. Every now and then the laughter of Bernard punctuated the steady drone of the sports caster:

"Hey sweetie, gimme a kiss come on! Hahaha, I like 'em with a little more spunk in 'em than you have kid. Hahaha. That stuff the Master hands out really makes 'em into zombies, right Ned? Hey Ned. Keep your eyes on the road. We don't want to have a wreck out here. And for god sakes take that disgusting mask off your face. I don't care if it makes you horny. Is it true that you skinned that off your own mother?"

"That's not true!" the old man behind the wheel said.

"Okay, okay, simmer down. But take that damned thing off. Thanks." said Bernard.

Now, Cy noticed the car making another left turn and heading south on Highway 14.

"We are heading south on Highway 14. We just turned at the Party House, the old Five Mile House Bar from pioneer days." said Cy.

"This is no time for a vest pocket history of La Crosse bars Cy." growled Monroe.

"Just trying to give you a fix on the location." Cy said.

"I think we are right behind you." said Monroe.

The car began to pick up speed after hitting Highway 14.

In a few minutes Cy realized they were climbing up into the hills.

"Still following Cy." said Monroe. "He is turning off I think. We will drop back a ways so he doesn't see us."

Sure enough, Bernard commented:

"Is that car following us Ned? Never mind. Keep your eyes on the road. Well, never mind. I think we lost him."

said Bernard.

"We'll follow the same road Cy, but out of their eyesight. Let us know if the car turns off somewhere."

"I think we are slowing down." Cy whispered into the radio after a bit.

And in a moment, the car came to a complete stop. Cy heard car doors open and close, and he heard people exit. Cautiously, he opened the trunk lid. At first, he saw nothing more than the vast star-strewn night sky. But gradually, his eyes could make out a large, empty farm field, no houses could be seen nearby. He could hear the footsteps of people walking into the field, away from the car. He quickly, quietly rolled out of the trunk and crouched on the ground next to the car. At the horizon he could see the figures of Bernard, Ned and Madeline, standing motionless and silent in the immense hay field.

Cy thought he could make out the approaching head lights of the Buick.

"Cut your lights out and park your car. I can see you coming. They probably could too if they looked this way. Come up here on foot. And get that gun out." Cy whispered into the radio.

Before long, Cy could hear the footfalls of Monroe and Philio as they climbed up the gravel road.

"What are they doing?" gasped Monroe, unaccustomed to physical exercise.

"Just standing way over there." said Cy. "Not doing anything."

"Maybe we should rush them before they get away." said Monroe.

At that exact moment, the entire field lit up brilliantly. A large inverted crescent or ark shaped object was suddenly visible in the field, not far from where Ned, Bernard and Madeline stood. A door was opening on the side of the object, which clearly seemed to be a manufactured craft of some kind. Presumably an aircraft, thought Cy (thinking quickly of the stories told him by Ken Starky).

The large Reptile being appeared in the doorway and walked down the ramp of the craft. He walked over to where Bernard, Ned and Madeline stood. Without a word, he took Madeline's hand and led her up the ramp of the vehicle. Monroe rushed forward:

"Halt! Madison Police Department. I'm placing you under arrest!" he shouted, brandishing his badge in one hand and his Colt .45 in the other. The tall, green creature calmly looked at Monroe and formed a sort of sneer with his shiny lips. He held up his right hand and a light beam came out of the palm of his hand, hit Monroe in the chest, and sent him flying to the ground. The creature turned and entered the craft with Madeline. The door closed behind them.

In another moment the ark shaped silver craft lifted majestically, silently from the hayfield, and in the blink of an eye vanished into the blackness of space.

"Well, I can get you two at least." said Cy, rushing over to pick up from the ground the gun of the inert Monroe. He pointed it at the face of Bernard.

"I would love to plug a hole in you, kid." Cy said.

Suddenly bright headlights came up the gravel road from both directions. Military jeeps swarmed along the road and into the field.

"Put that gun down Mr. Butt." said an Army officer who strode into the field, flanked by other, younger officers and followed by a squadron of rifle-toting infantry.

"This is a classified security area as of now, Mr. Butt. You and your friends are in our custody."

"What about those two? What about that poor girl being hauled off by that snake man in that flying saucer." Cy pleaded.

"That is none of your affair, Mr. Butt. We will take care of the entire matter. Please come along quietly."

A jeep pulled up along the road. Sitting in the rear seat were the Master and the blond lawyer from La Crosse.

EPILOGUE
Saturday, October 31, 1953,
Madison, Wis.

P hilio DeGarmo drove his new, blue colored, 1953 Hudson Hornet up East Washington Avenue in Madison, heading toward the Wisconsin State Capitol building, resplendent in its floodlit gleam of early evening Halloween, as Attorney General Grover W. Townsend and Cy Butt sat in the back seat, recounting the details of the recent case:

"Cy, we can rest assured that although the Master has not actually been apprehended and brought to justice, that some Federal authorities now believe us when we send them reports of this criminal conspiracy." intoned Grover, gazing up at the white domed structure with a faraway look in his eyes.

"Grover, it seems to me that the Feds know a great deal more about this man than they are letting on" said Cy.

"Well, we have all been cautioned not to speak about

this matter anymore." Grover glanced meaningfully at Philio, who nodded quickly to his boss. "But I do want to express my sincere thanks for helping us. And I'm sorry for any....difficulties you may have encountered up there at the Army base at Camp McCoy. If I had known how complicated things were I wouldn't have asked you to get involved."

"No problem Grover. I love a good adventure. Most of the time I have not much to do, and no place to go. And at least Philio here got a new car out of the deal" said Cy, with a cackle, looking from one man to another with his searing gaze. Both men refrained from comment. Philio coughed slightly from the front seat--perhaps as a warning to Cy.

"I think Monroe Hammersley might be a wee bit less amenable to your kind words, however." said Cy, with a swallowed chuckle.

Grover coughed, wearily: "Yes, well. He is being taken care of...financially."

"He will like that." said Cy.

"Yes, he will. By the way, he has a message for you Cy" said Grover.

"What is it?" Cy replied.

"Something about where you should put your damned canned soup." said Grover. "He got quite specific in terms of his suggestions. I won't ask." he continued.

Cy laughed but could not resist another gibe: "What you going to get out of all this Grover? The governorship of Wisconsin? Hmmmmm? Well, you deserve it." And then he settled into an infrequent, respectful silence.

"Tell me, Grover, doesn't it really bug you that these men get off Scot free and they seem to have powerful backers." asked Cy, more in a thoughtful than an outraged manner.

"Yes, of course it does Cy. I just have to place my trust in the Eternal and in the belief that He will place His hand upon the hearts of the leaders of our land. I also trust that the information our government obtains from these creatures makes what we have...endured...to be worthwhile." intoned Grover.

And the car rolled past the capitol building, turning right on State Street. Cy began to study the Halloween-clad college students beginning their night time revel. Fraternity and sorority types were garbed as ghosts and ghouls, witches and Wisconsin badgers. Disorganized band units drummed and trumpeted and tooted throughout the crowd.

"Incidentally, young lawyer Prentiss has vacated his apartment in Viroqua, leaving no forwarding address. All his landlord said was that an official Army car stopped by and Prentiss and his suitcases were loaded up and driven away by a soldier in uniform. The lawyer in La Crosse also seems to have left that city for some mysterious long term stay. Even the desk clerk at the Hotel Grant has disappeared. " added Grover.

Cy just exchanged looks with Grover and finally shook his head.

"Well, at least Professor Alterweise is out of the hospital. That would have been a great loss, not only to me, but to this city if they had succeeded in killing him." said Cy.

"He's where you got that key to that corridor isn't it Cy?" asked Philio, grinning at Cy through the rear view mirror.

"I told you Philio, that I cannot and will not say,"

said Cy with a grin. "Please drop me off down at Nino's Bar on University Avenue, would you, Philio?" asked Cy.

"Sure thing Cy." said Philio, looking back at his passengers in the back seat through the rear view mirror.

"Cy ..." said Grover pulling a white business-sized envelope out of his coat pocket. "...here's a little something for your...expenses."

"Thanks, Grover."

"Don't mention it Cy. And I really mean that quite literally... don't mention it, ever." Grove gave Cy a serious gaze which the *bon vivant* found mildly uncomfortable.

Somewhere down the street a band had coalesced out of the crowd of revelers. They played *On Wisconsin.*

ABOUT THE AUTHOR

John H. Sime, born 1952, Viroqua, Wis.; graduated in
Comparative Literature BA/MA from University of
Wisconsin-Madison 74/76; served U.S. Peace Corps in
Mali, West Africa, teacher at École Normale Supérieure
teachers college in Bamako, Mali 76-78; graduated
Kentucky School of Mortuary Science, Louisville,
Kentucky 1980; funeral director in Western Wisconsin;
published in: Kickapoo Free Press, Wisconsin Poets
Calendar, Verse Wisconsin, Lake City Lights,
Hummingbird, American Funeral Director magazine,
Poetry Motel, LaFarge Epitaph News, Crawford County
Independent, Kickapoo Scout, and the Broadcaster
Censor.

www.ingramcontent.com/pod-product-compliance
Lightning Source LLC
Chambersburg PA
CBHW071223260626
47162CB00004B/1408